Sword, Wand & Rainbow

Yvonne Li
Elaine Li

Tellwell Talent
www.tellwell.ca

ISBN
978-0-2288-4971-1 (Hardcover)
978-0-2288-4970-4 (Paperback)

For our parents, who introduced us to the wonderful world of books at a very young age, who encouraged us to make reading and writing our favorite hobbies, and who taught us the virtues of hard working and perseverance.

For our grandparents, who devote all their time and energy to taking care of our daily lives meticulously.

And for Professor Ashton Howley, our friend and tutor, who enlightened us with classic literature and empowered us with the skill of creative writing.

Imaginus Scribimus

We are perishing for want of wonder,
not for want of wonders.
—*G. K. Chesterton*

Imaginus Scribimus (in Latin, "imagine we write") is a collection of twenty-eight stories, thirty-two essays, and six poems authored by two sisters—Yvonne (age eight) and Elaine (age seven), adorned by the sketches **of artist's name** that inspire vividness in readers' imagination. A glance at the Table of Contents reveals the diversity of the authors' interests, their essays encompassing a wide array of subjects that explore light-hearted topics such as cooking, homeschooling, plant growing, creative vs. academic writing, the library, learning, and education; and also serious concerns: climate change, civil rights, Covid-19, mask wearing, health, antismoking, bullying, unethical zoos, habitat preservation for endangered species, nature vs. technology, and fear of death, among others. Their poems, by contrast, engage, in even merrier tones, the less intense subject matter of seasonal holidays (Thanksgiving, Christmas), raft-building, a recipe for friendship, and feelings of the heart. Their stories' splendid array of colorful characters **include range from** harmless dragons in need of math lessons, shapeshifting trolls, greedy elves, now-to-the-rescue robots, and magical fairies along with the familiar archetypes of Queens and Kings, Princesses and Princes, "and so many more," as the elder author puts it.

Content aside for a moment, readers will admire the quality of the writing that awaits their perusal. These young authors are probably already better writers than most of their readers. Advanced sentences abounding (absolute phrases, appositives, resumptive and summative modifiers, cumulative adjectives lined up properly without commas, to name just a few of their adept turns of phrase) inscribe their clever verbal wanderings.

Needless to say, this compilation offers delightful reading experiences, and not just for kids. Adults can also unearth valuable gems in the literature these authors have composed, literature that partakes of its own genre, that of literature written by and/or for kids.

As Alison Laurie writes, in *Don't Tell the Grown Ups: The Subversive Power of Children's Literature* (1990), this genre tends to "mock current assumptions and express the imaginative, unconventional, noncommercial view of the world in its simplest and purest form. It appeals to the imaginative, questioning, rebellious child within all of us, renews our instinctive energy, and acts as a force for change." One lesson offered by the authors of this collection motivates readers to accept the irrational in life. Many a sharp turn or sudden twist occurring in the plots of their stories might strike some readers as violations of good sense, unconventional at best or at worst illogical, as they wonder at the robot appearing in a Medieval setting to help the distressed princess or raise an eyebrow at nerdy dragons enjoying math lessons. However, the surprising occurrences of their identified *errata* are hardly misplaced in the realm of post-toddler imagination into which the willing reader will delightfully be drawn.

The editor of this collection observed that some of their stories "start with one problem and then take a turn," such that "the original problem is never resolved." "For an adult author," the editor writes, "I would advise on fixing this so there is a proper narrative progression." The editor then refuses to impose an adult's sensibility on the sisters' creativity: as "the authors are two children ... it's perfectly acceptable and even preferrable to leave the stories as adorably nonsensical." The editor's decision goes against a longstanding trend of altering children's stories for rational reasons. "For nearly two hundred years" (Lurie, 1990, p. 20), unacknowledged changes have been made in the original **texts.**" Editors "often speed up the appearance of the woodsman so that he walks in just after the villain has growled his immortal last line, 'The better to eat you with, my dear!'" (p. 22), as an example. For Laurie, these sorts of alterations pull the blinds down on gleeful irrationalities, flattening the drama of the tales—reducing their appeal, their amusement, and even their insightfulness. She cites psychoanalyst Bruno Bettelheim's *Uses of Enchantment* (1976) to say that children's literature promotes the irrational, the magical, and the mysterious, all integral to the development of a healthy imagination. Such promotion, maturing, nurtured over time becomes integral in adults to "soul-making," in the words of James Hillman, for whom intellectual growth is at its best for those who retain this childlike sense of wonder toward the universe, one that is as natural to human fulfillment "as wetness to water, as motion to wind" (*Re-Visioning Psychology*, 1977, p. 117).

The editors of this collection have, then, decided—wisely, in my opinion—to leave intact elements that others less attuned to one of the most charming features of the genre might have altered for sake of adherence to the literary norms of "narrative progression." In their doing so, the valuable lesson that this collection's writings offer adult readers is preserved—the joy of childhood discoveries that incite astonishment at the irrational and unexpected occurrences in our lives. The remarkable literature generated by these young authors will doubtlessly prove entertaining to young readers, too (those who are not likely reading this introduction). To adult readers, however, it offers lessons that most of us need to re-learn since much of adult discovery is hindered by the biases and blindness of opinion acquired over time whose inexorable passage feeling like so much shortness of breath, we become oblivious to the buried content cast into the soft concrete of our youth, concealed, congealed, cataracted. Kids' fresh discoveries, by contrast, are unencumbered by such restraints. Adults "leave the tribal culture of childhood behind ... lose contact with instinctive joy in self-expression: with the creative imagination, spontaneous emotion, and the ability to see the world as full of wonders"

(Lurie, 1990). Her comment is reminiscent of Carl Jung's observation, in "The Psychology of the Child Archetype," that stories embodying the archetype of the irrational, spontaneous child "have a vital meaning. Not merely do they represent, they *are* the psychic life of the primitive tribe" (*Psyche and Symbol*, 1958, p. 128), the "real but invisible roots" of human consciousness (p. 134). Returning to childhood in the form of reexperiencing childlike awareness is, for Jung, an "original form of *religio* ('linking back') ...the essence, the working basis of all religious life even today, and will always be, whatever future form this life may take" (135).

These observations on the links between childhood and a rich imagination are rooted in Romanticism, whose English mantra was coined by poet laureate William Wordsworth in 1798. The "spontaneous overflow" of emotion that he celebrated in children's creativity makes them, in some ways, wiser than their parents—"the child is the father of the man," as he famously put it later in "My Heart Leaps Up" (1808). However, the "shades of the prison house begin to close upon the growing" child ("Tintern Abbey," 1798), the shades being the processes of maturity. The sentiment is common in commentaries on the links between childhood and creativity and on the lack thereof in adulthood. "Every child is an artist," runs Picasso's oft-cited remark. "The problem is how to remain an artist once [one] grows up" (*Time Magazine*, 1976). The sentiment is echoed in Nietzsche's remark, that maturity means "regain[ing] the seriousness" one had "as a child at play" (*Beyond Good and Evil*, 1989). This emphasis on kids' emotional and imaginative spontaneousness goes hand in hand with a de-emphasis of the rational, a concept that the following stories, essays, and poems embody so adorably, their value residing in their power to demonstrate what most adults have lost or misplaced over the years of gaining experience: the spontaneous, irrational imagination that Wordsworth and the others cited above find essential to our leading meaningful lives.

The authors of this collection, for example, do not "muddle" their heads by having to "imagine a necessary mental connection between a horn and a falling tower," to borrow terms from G. K. Chesterton's "The Ethics of Elfland" (*Orthodoxy*, 1908). They embody the "peculiar perfection of tone and truth" that we can find in the genre of children's literature. "The man of science says, 'Cut the stalk, and the apple will fall.' But the man of science 'says it calmly, as if the one idea really led up to the other.' The witch in the fairy tale says, 'Blow the horn, and the ogre's castle will fall'; but she does not say it as if it were something in which the effect obviously arose out of the cause."

Chesterton offers useful insights about the timeless value that children's tales have for adults. He offers two principles for our contemplation: (1) the common sense of "Fairyland," a special kind of logic that instills in readers "a certain way of looking at life," one that restores in readers an "elementary wonder"—the "ancient instinct of astonishment"; and (2) the "Doctrine of Conditional Joy." Consider, he says, the shift occurring between toddlerdom and later childhood: whereas "[a] child of seven is excited by being told that Tommy opened a door and saw a dragon, a child of three is excited by being told that Tommy opened a door .... These tales say that apples were golden only to refresh the forgotten moment when we found that they were green. They make rivers run with wine only to make us remember, for one wild moment, that they run with water."

The antonym of familiarity is astonishment Restoring primitive feelings felt when first experiencing elements of life's splendor sustains wonder in human existence, an effect further inspired by Chesterton's second principle. Often in children's literature, he writes, "happiness depended on NOT DOING SOMETHING which you could at any moment do and which, very often, it was not obvious why you should not do.... A box is opened, and all evils fly out. A word is forgotten, and cities perish. A lamp is lit, and love flies away." For Chesterton, this

"Doctrine of Conditional Joy" frustrates the adult tendency to protest the unreasonable. However, for him, "the point here ... did not seem unjust. If the miller's third son said to the fairy, 'Explain why I must not stand on my head in the fairy palace,' the other might fairly reply, 'Well, if it comes to that, explain the fairy palace.'" The irrational nature of children's stories ultimately resides in their capacity to make us see this "truth": "existence was itself so very eccentric a legacy that [we cannot] complain of not understanding the limitations of the vision when [we do] not understand the vision they limited. The frame was no stranger than the picture ("The Ethics of Elfland," 1908).

Reading this collection of stories, essays, and poems means—to borrow once more from Lurie—not just "understanding what children are thinking and feeling; it is a way of understanding and renewing our own childhood" (p. 204). The vision that emerges in this treasury is pristine in both its portrayal and its preservation of childhood imagination unfraught by the restraints of reason. As photographs of moments of our childhoods capture forgotten memories, so this unique collection's showcasing of these *littérateurs'* perceptions of the world in the first decade of their lives issues significant reminders to us all: let's find wonder in existence, let's return to our early perceptions through the time machine of imagination, rendering the familiar new and the new familiar—Chesterton again—and let's delight in life's sudden twists and turns. So runs the cliché: *the one constant in life is change.*

—Ashton Howley, PhD

References

Chesterton, G.K (1908). *Orthodoxy.* New York: Dodd, Mead & Co., 1908
    WEB: https://www.ccel.org/ccel/chesterton/orthodoxy.vii.html

Hillman, James. Re-visioning Psychology (1977). New York: Harper and Row (1975), p. 117.

Jung, C.G (1991, 1958). Psyche and Symbol: A Selection from the Writings of C.G. Jung. Trans. R.F.C. Hull. Selected and introduced by Violet S. de Lazlo. New Jersey: Princeton University Press.

Lurie, A. (1990). Don't Tell the Grown-Ups: The Subversive Power of Children's Literature. New York: Little, Brown and Company.

Nietzsche, F. (1989). *Beyond* Good and Evil: A Prelude to the Philosophy of the Future. New York: Vintage Press.

Picasso, P (1976). The quotation appears as an epigraph at the beginning of the article. (Online archive of Time magazine. Date: October 4, 1976, Periodical: Time, Article: Modern Living: Ozmosis in Central Park.

Wordsworth, W. (1798). Tintern Abbey reference

Ashton Howley holds a PhD from the University of Ottawa as a recipient of the Research Council of Canada Doctoral fellowship and has taught American literature, children's literature, and literature and psychology at various universities, colleges, and institutions in Canada and Korea. His publications in The Journal of Modern Literature and with Palgrave Macmillan Press, among others, explore issues of gender, psychology, philosophy, and aesthetics in the works of various authors. Scribo Writers, Inc. is his online teaching school attended by kids and adults both in Canada and abroad.

Table of Contents

Part 1: Stories by Yvonne

Griffin Story

Once there lived a griffin who supported the life of a castle that belonged to a king, a queen, and a princess. The griffin had two golden wings and red and yellow ravishing feathers that fell as she flew. The griffin's name was Lavender and she never broke a promise. In the castle, the king was named Robert, and he had a super bad issue. The griffin had just disappeared this morning, and even though he searched everywhere, the griffin was nowhere to be found. Only a single clue was hidden on Princess Rosie's shelf. A gold and red feather lay there near a scratch—not a scratch that Lavender had made. No one knew what mysterious creature had made the scratch. As the kingdom struggled and struggled to keep working and supporting each other, the king's brother heard this news, invited them to his wealthy castle, and promised to support them there. But it was not an easy task since there was a bridge they had to cross which had a monster living under it that no one could destroy.

As the king, queen, and princess set off to travel, the castle was overtaken by a witch who had worked for a creature that had never been seen. However, the princess was smarter than anyone thought. She quietly took a path that was a shortcut to her uncle's castle. Once there, she told that whole castle about the issue and then set off on a journey to see the greatest wizard of all the land, who was also known as the most powerful person in the land and was able to create an army and find the creature who took the griffin—all by herself.

Rosie returned to the group as soon as she knew she had to set her plan in motion later since wasting a bunch of strong men for an army would be a terrible idea. When Robert finally reached the bridge, the monster was ready to pounce, but before anyone could move, the king pulled out a glove, but not an ordinary glove. This glove had the power to control whatever creature and whatever person was nearby. So as the king slowly crawled to the creature, he made it sleep until it was one thousand years old, and that was more than a year, so they set off toward the castle. After Princess Rosie explained every issue to Robert's brother, she went to the garden and found a rusty golden key hidden among the rose bush. So, she carefully took it and when she touched it, a giant evil robot stood in front of her.

Instead of attacking, the robot just said, "Answer five riddles and then you can pass to the queen's castle."

Rosie was surprised that a robot would make suggestions instead of attacking, but she quietly nodded and put her thinking cap on since she really wasn't good at riddles.

"First riddle," chimed the robot. "What has a forest but no trees, cities but no people, and rivers but no water?"

Rosie was lucky she had a cousin. She remembered that her cousin once asked her that riddle.

"A map!"

"Correct," beeped the robot. "Next: I can only live where there is light, but if the light shines on me, I die."

Rosie saw that the sun was out and saw her shadow. When she walked directly to the light, it disappeared, so she bellowed, "A shadow!"

"Correct again, miss. Next: how can you make seven even without using subtraction or any other math."

Rosie knew this was a trick question since it is impossible if you really don't think that much.

"Umm, you take away the 's'?"

"Correct. You have shown that you have a smart brain and that you are wise enough to defeat anything, so I will let you pass even though we didn't do five riddles, but remember, your majesty, a creature is following your path, so be very wise and make smart choices."

As Rosie tiptoed to the entrance of the cave, she saw that in the very middle in front of her was a guard! This guard was a huge spider with big hairy legs, red beady eyes, and huge fangs dripping with poison—a monster spider who could eat her alive! The good news was that it was sound asleep and that even its fangs were sucked into its mouth. Rosie carefully approached it and wondered how she could get past it because it was so vast that it covered most of the spacious hall.

She found a ladder that reached the roof, a string that was almost unbreakable, and super glue that she found in her pocket. So, silently and rapidly, she set the ladder up and climbed each rung with a wild mind. Then she took her super glue and stuck some to the wall. And finally, she took the unbreakable string and held it there for five minutes. As she carefully put the ladder away, she climbed up the unbreakable string and started to swing. With a mighty push, she swung to the very edge of the spider and jumped down in perfect timing behind the queen, since the queen was wondering why she could feel vibrations on the floor. As Rosie carefully turned around to see she was facing the queen, she realized it wasn't a queen really. It was a vampire!

She screamed a scream in pure terror and took off running down the stairs, not knowing where she was going—that was the way to the dungeon and she had to go back to get out as a whole army was heading for her! She quickly hid behind the door, and when the queen vampire came, she knocked her to the ground and quickly rifled out the keys from her dress and rapidly locked herself in the biggest dungeon with the keys and closed the door, making sure that it was locked.

When the army came to search for the queen, they found out that Rosie was in the cell and were calling the key maker to make the exact same key so they could unlock the cell and get her. While the army was doing this, she dressed like the queen vampire and started to sit on the throne, when suddenly, the door burst open.

"Just in time," Rosie said because the army was back.

In her best vampire tone, she ordered each of all the army leaders to a meeting. Rosie made the meeting about changing them into an army fighting on behalf of the good. If anyone did one wrong move, they would get five detentions for a day for at least two hours. She ordered all of them to walk out of the cave and reappear at the garden. Then she went out and told King Robert and his brother what had happened. They asked the army if they could defeat the monster. As the army solemnly nodded their heads no, they asked the army if they could persuade it to help them find the creature who took the griffin. With a slight smile, the army went to the monster and woke him up.

"Just toque ma no se do ma trose?"

And the army showed the monster a ring more precious than gold and more beautiful than jewels. The monster quickly glanced at it and agreed with a quick nod. The army, the royal family, and the monster set off to the most terrible island of them all, where of course the creature would be hiding. On their way to the island, they found a dragon resting on a rock.

"Gabriella!" yelled Rosie.

She introduced the pink and orange dragon who was nuzzling Rosie the whole time.

"How many kilometres do we have left?"

"Thirty-five," said Robert.

"This is our lucky day!" said Rosie, and then she commanded, "Hop on, people. We are going to fly twenty-five kilometres and meet my dear bear friend there who can carry us five kilometres, and then we can walk the rest of the way!"

So all of the creatures and people hopped on and Gabriella took off. When they reached their destination, they started to walk upward on the path, but then Rosie whistled a high pitch song and out came a big black bear.

"Hello, Blackberry!" chimed Rosie as she went on with the others.

Halfway through, they found a skunk and a bundle of berries.

"Shhh," cried Rosie.

So, the crew quietly tiptoed past the skunk and rapidly stole the berries. As Rosie built a fire, the monster taught Robert how to make blueberry cake and cherry pie. Rosie gave some to Blackberry, and they set off again. When they reached their destination, Rosie thanked Blackberry and started walking. *Huff, puff, huff, puff.* The whole group was exhausted from walking and were fast asleep on the floor. When the group woke up, they were already at the island! And right in front of them was where the queen was living! A black castle.

The crew slowly walked in and found Lavender on the floor, sleeping. And right in front of them was the creature who stole the griffin. It was a great black cobra with five heads!

"Who are you?" hissed the snake.

"We have come to take the griffin back from you," said Rosie as she took a stroll toward it.

"Mmmm, brave princesssssss."

"I am King Robert, and why have you taken our griffin that supports our kingdom?" demanded Robert.

"Our kingdomsssss have relationshipsssss, they both need the griffin to sssssupport each other'sssssss kingdomssssss."

The whole time that the group was talking, the monster and the army made the ring tell the group that they should jump on the griffin and ride on her back while they defeated the snake. So, they quickly paused their sentence and jumped onto the griffin who was already prepared to fly. And instead of fighting, the monster just told the ring to bring them with the group that just left. And in a minute, they were flying with them all on separate unicorns. When the adventurers arrived home, they lived ineffably ever after.

THE END

Cherryscent and the Kingdom of Magic

Once there lived a fairy named Cherryscent who supported a whole kingdom of magic. Cherryscent was a sweet, beautiful, and kind fairy who always had the power to turn evil to good unless the evil was powered by the Serpent of Evil.

One morning, Cherryscent decided to go to the trolls of Trolley, a huge tree where trolls lived. All the trolls used to live with the Serpent of Evil, but once they decided to run away, Cherryscent collected them and made them a nice home to comfort the trolls. That was how the kingdom knew how the Serpent of Evil treated his guests and prisoners.

Cherryscent reached the huge tree and found a huge bundle of trolls lying on the ground, dead. Blood was everywhere and the tree was so demolished it couldn't be repaired by Cherryscent's magic. The stunned Cherryscent walked silently as she made her way through the bundles of trolls. She heard a rustle. Then she saw the only troll who had survived was walking toward her and his hands were covered with bleeding blisters.

"What happened?" asked Cherryscent as silent tears gathered in her eyes.

"The Serpent of Evil came and killed everyone, but I hid in a tunnel which he couldn't fit into."

Cherryscent gaped while her tears departed and rolled down her rosy cheeks which turned white and pale.

"We must go to the Waterfall of Wizards to see the future and change it by means of an exchange with a snow fairy. Then we must go to the Cave of Coaxing Crystals and give a diamond to them so we can change the future."

The troll looked hopeful, but a twinkle of sadness settled in his eyes.

"Okay," the troll said as he went back in the tree to gather all the supplies and food and clothing he needed, so as not to have to worry about suffering any conditions or running out of food.

Cherryscent stood staring at the demolished tree and slowly turned around to go back to the kingdom to tell everyone the heartbreaking news.

"Oh no!" cried Cherryscent's husband as he took her hand and looked her straight in the eyes. "Oh why do we have to do this?" said her husband as Cherryscent told him her plan.

"We must do it. It is our only chance to win our side and to defeat the Serpent of Evil. This is the shortest way according to the map of our whole country."

Cherryscent sighed and suddenly felt hot tears in her eyes again, tears that started to burst as she wondered what caused the Serpent of Evil to come back and destroy the Kingdom of Fantasy.

"Okay, I will alert the whole kingdom and bring the strongest and smartest soldiers to a meeting about training. Give us two weeks to train as hard as we can, so we can be prepared to defeat the Serpent of Evil."

Cherryscent, weak and sad, smiled, and her smile was still filled with hope. She turned around to go alert the people in the castle and tell them to gather all the things they needed.

Once Cherryscent finally got everyone moving and getting their clothing, food, and furniture, they went discussing what was the best type of transportation they should use because the Waterfall of Wizards was really far, and no people from such kingdoms had gone there yet. Only the greatest had gone there, only those already dead because they were only a legend, ancient role models of all the people in their kingdom.

"Everyone, attention!" yelled Cherryscent as she took a vote about which transportation was best. "Raise your hand if we should go in a carriage."

No hands went up. Only the children's did, the hands of those who loved to be in carriages, so all the children who lived in the Kingdom of Fantasy raised their hands and started giggling.

"Raise your hand if we should go in airplanes."

No hands went up because airplanes came from the real world, and they didn't like real-world things. Not from the Kingdom of Fantasy. They also disliked going in an airplane because it always made them dizzy, no matter how hard they tried to be comfortable, which is also really common in the real world.

"Raise your hand to go in the Unicorns of Charity."

All the hands, including Cherryscent's hand, went up.

"It is settled then. We will travel using the Unicorns of Charity."

Cherryscent put her hands in her mouth and whistled a unique and beautiful tune. Suddenly, a bunch of unicorns flew down from the sky.

"Children, you will ride on the young ponies named Bloom, Skylight, Moontwinkle, Strawberry Cake, Twinkle Dust, and Sunglow. The adult unicorns will be the ones close up to the gate by the chariots."

Cherryscent climbed onto her own sparkly unicorn and bellowed, "Pet your unicorn's mane and it will fly."

Everyone did as Cherryscent said and took off in the direction of the Waterfall of Wizards.

"We are here!" sang Cherryscent as everyone was looking at a sparkly waterfall with rainbow water pouring down the glittering white rocks.

Everyone stepped forward and oohed at the great sight of the Kingdom of Fantasy from their elevated perspective.

"Let's go!" said Cherryscent as she skipped past everyone and uncovered a huge purple slide that went down the waterfall without getting you wet.

Cherryscent then sat and slid down and yelled back, "Slide down and meet me at the end!"

Everyone stumbled and went on it all at once, so when they were at the end, a few people still got wet.

"We are here," said Cherryscent as everyone watched a bunch of Wizards saying a spell.

Whirling and twirling, put your wand in a box.
Say this magic spell to turn into a fox.
Whisker of a tiger, half a dead lizard.
A spider's arm, part of a wizard.
An elephant's tusk, a human's tummy.
A dog's leg, guts from a mummy.
Stir the mixture with part of a feather—
It will make you sing forever.

"Ahem, can we please trade a change in the future for a magic snow fairy."

The oldest wizard stopped whatever chant he was making.

"Of course, your majesty," said the wizard as he bowed awkwardly.

Cherryscent put her hand tightly around her wand and started to chant a spell that made a magical snow fairy be born.

This was what Cherryscent chanted:

A snow draft thickens and growth becomes goal.
The pace now quickens as I turn within my soul.
The last days of cold, winter growing old.
I'm ready to embark beyond this nightly and daily dark.
I advance my soul, my body and mind.
Seeking within to see what I shall find.
I ignite under the light of the moon.
For my spiritual journey shall be in tune.

A sparkly young snow fairy appeared on the wizard's hand. The rest of this story is unknown here but known to anyone currently living on Mars.

THE END

A Locket From Someone Loved

Down in the deep, scary woods lived a cruel, evil, wicked, sinister, and diabolical creature named Scumpy Underwear who was a shapeless creature of the dark. She had the power to act like a shape-shifter, which means that she was able to change into anybody and any shape, no matter what. So, BEWARE!!! She tends to adore rattling the windows of children who don't believe in monsters, dark magic or wickedness. She also likes to create love potions and other potions too.

One day, Scumpy felt like taking over the world because what's the point of someone being cruel and hiding in a deep forest doing nothing but just making potions? What's the point of that? So, Scumpy set out on an adventure to find the ingredients for the world's most valuable potion.

She would need:

A branch from the youngest tree in the world
A locket from someone adored
Water from the bluest sea
One minute under a full moon

Scumpy started her adventure around the forest since that was the only place that had the most important trees. Once in a while, she walked and walked and walked. She was so busy looking at the trees that she was not looking where she was going and tripped on a big root. When she finally got up and brushed herself off, she realized that the root she had tripped on was a branch from the youngest tree in the world! She picked it up and stuffed it in her bag. Now she had to find someone she adores, a task difficult for her since she adored no one!

"Wait a minute," she uttered.

She knew that she adored herself, so she could just go in her house and cut a locket from a necklace. Scumpy went into her cabin. While she did so, a burglar was robbing her house. At the first sight of the necklace, he took it and stuffed it in his pocket. While he was looking for other things to rob, he sang a poem about things he needed.

This is what he sang:

"Bread, bread, wonderful bread, the most things I ever need!"

Scumpy was furious and hid under her bed till she saw the invader who was in her cabin. This dwarf's name was Pimpleskiln! When he took the necklace out of his pocket, Scumpy desperately wanted to turn into a fearful monster and take the necklace back. Instead, she pulled out her notebook and started to write down things he wore and what he looked like.

She wrote that the dwarf:

Is very stubby-looking
Has a very long and yellow beard
Is very greedy
Wears red pants and a green shirt
Isn't nice at all
Has short brown, curly hair
Has rainbow shoes

Scumpy then transformed into a mouse, and instead of running away, she was face to face with a gigantic robot!

This was what he said in robot mode:

"I am a robot. Is there anything I can do for you?"

"Yes, I do need you to help me. Can you take that necklace away from that silly dwarf and hand it to me?"

"Of course," the robot replied and rolled straight to the dwarf, grabbed it away from him and disappeared with a big WOOSH.

The necklace and a pair of scissors were in front of Scumpy, so she grabbed it, cut it, and turned into a blue jay and flew away. The dwarf was set in a very deep dungeon, Scumpy's grandma's dungeon called PinPin prison. The creature was so astonished, he fainted and never got up.

Scumpy paused her trip to take a vacation to Las Vegas to relax. How fancy! After that vacation, it was Christmas! When Scumpy got home from Las Vegas, she found her presents waiting to be opened at her dinner table. She tore the wrappers off her presents and guess what was waiting to be opened as a present?

It was:

A big bag of rubies
A glowing mirror
Jewels from a crown
An umbrella

Scumpy was very satisfied once she saw her presents when suddenly she heard a *rustle rustle* behind her Christmas tree! She transformed into a mouse and scurried to the Christmas tree. She slowly and carefully opened it with her sharp teeth and guess what it was? It was the dwarf who had just escaped PinPin prison all by himself!

Scumpy was furious, so furious that she turned into an Orgulg, picked him up, and threw him right out of her cabin and broke her window with a CRASH and a BANG! Now the dwarf was furious and came crashing through the wood and was about to grab a death potion and spill it on her, but it was too late. That was the story of Pimpleskiln's death.

His grave site says:

This dwarf was a smart little fellow, you know
He could weave hay into gold and
Buckle up his old shoe
In a snap of his fingers.
In shame, he fell
To death by a horrible shape-shifter
Named Scumpy Underwear!

THE END

Dwarfs–Greedy!

There used to live a gang of greedy dwarfs named Mori, Hifur, Nofur, Wombur, Lili, Mili, and last but not least, Zago. All these dwarfs had pointy ears, little noses and yellow teeth. They lived in a cave full of gold and food. All of these dwarfs had something special about them. Mori could breathe underwater, Hifur could eat like a panda, Nofur could read people's minds, Wombur could steal a lot of jewellery, Lili could have the power to be like a shape-shifter, Mili could make weapons in one second and Zago could hypnotize people to do whatever he wanted them to do. This special gang of dwarfs were skilled with their powers. Even though you would think that they were unbeatable, they only had one enemy.

It was... the gang of elves! There were eight elves, all of them having special powers too. All of the elves' names were: Whitestorm, Cravenpaw, Budclaw, Bitestorm, Gluestar, Spottedoaf, Lirestar and Mloudtail. These elves were from a castle full of food and riches.

These two gangs used to be friends, but now they weren't. The story is this:

There once lived a family of dwarfs and elves. One day, the dwarfs decided to see who was the strongest. All the dwarfs or all the elves. They decided to play a prank on the elves. Nori swam under the sea and found a half-shark, half-dog animal. He used this animal to fight against all the elves. This animal was scandalously strong. He could take your head off in a second. All the dwarfs were very pleased with him. They all named him THE ETERNALLY GREAT AND AMAZING Ashton.

Once he noticed that his name was Ashton, he started yelping and peeing on his head. Before the dwarfs could do anything else, he fainted, followed by a big disgusting fart! Within another second, all the dwarfs started to complain. Within yet another second, all the elves came rushing in to see where all the fuss came from. All of the dwarfs looked at the elves glumly. The dwarfs slowly pulled their weapons out, and in a flash, the elves and the dwarfs were fighting.

Suddenly the elves ran away in fear. And the dwarfs cheered for joy knowing that they were stronger than the elves. But, still. This family was separated for now and then... forever. The end. Well, not really the end. That was the story about how the dwarfs got separated from the elves.

One day, the dwarfs wanted to meet the elves again in battle! They knew where to go, but it was going to be a long trip. First, they had to bring along some bags, bags filled with food such as ice cream, chocolate, pineapples, bananas, watermelons, oranges, tomatoes, soup, ice, peas, peaches, candy, sticks, vegetables, hot sauce, corn, and wheat. They also brought jackets, water bottles, blankets, pillows, and of course, way more! Now they were ready.

While they were walking, Mori spotted something. It was a bag. He opened it, and his eyes grew wide! He explained that the bag they found belonged to Gluestar! Mori went on his knees and sniffed the whole way till they reached the elves' castle. All of the dwarfs' eyes popped out of their sockets when they saw the elves' castle. The thing that caused them to envy the elves' castle was that it was made out of candy! All of the dwarfs quickly took a piece of candy and stuffed it in their mouths.

But this castle was actually made out of poison! So, all of the dwarfs fell down. Well don't think that they were dead. They just fainted! Once they got up, they found themselves surrounded by all the elves, including their family members! Within another minute, they were thrown into jail. While they got there, they realized that Wombur was missing. They searched for Wombur all over the prison, but there was no sight of him. Wombur actually escaped from the elves, and he was planning to get the jail keys to free his brothers. He snuck into the king elf's bathroom and took a bath. Then he put on the king's clothes, and since he knew how the king elf looked, he made a wig to look like him. Then he got out of the bathroom and asked for the jail keys. He slid silently down the hall once he got the keys and quickly opened the jail doors to let his brothers escape.

THE END

Elsanna: Queen of the Alicorns

Some unique horses once lived in the Land of Rainbow Ravishing Horses. Of the several types of horses, the first ones were called alicorns: very special and fragile little creatures who had special powers to protect themselves from their enemies. Another special horse was the Pegasus: a kind of horse that could fly very high into the sky. The Pegasus had powerful wings that let them fly away from other things that could be harmful for them. Pegasusses also had powers that were almost identical to alicorns. Lastly, the littlest but specialist of horses, unicorns, were unique because of their clever minds. They could trick a witch who had a clever wolf partner. A unicorn could also have the same powers as an alicorn and Pegasus. Unicorns had strong colourful wings, outstanding powers, and clever minds, so basically a unicorn was an intensely fragile horse and didn't look so pretty and powerful.

There lived a powerful alicorn named Elsanna, the Queen of Alicorns. Her husband was named Eric who usually had the same job as Elsanna, so mostly he protected her. Elsanna had a sister who was also a queen and was the only Pegasus that could fly higher than all the rest of the special horses. Her name was Lolo. Her husband's name was Ashtonio who was a very weak horse and a terrible writer who was fired from being king since Lolo found him bullying a little Pegasus, so she fired him and decided to choose another husband soon. And last but not least was the Queen of Unicorns. There stood a very enchanting, ravishing, attractive, and powerful unicorn named Star Light.

All of these enchanting horses lived on only one island. Near them there was a waterfall called the Waterfalls of Wizards, since when it was pouring water down, they blended the waters with different coloured stars that contained power for the wizards who live in this land. The power from the stars may have seemed fragile. The stars protected the wizards by gaining power that harmful enemies cannot face. These two islands had been friends ever since. All the special horses had at least met all of the wizards two times!

One day, Elsanna decided to create a special holiday that included all the wizards in the Waterfalls of Wizards. The activities you had to do for this holiday were to relax! There were games and places where you can watch TV and do nothing at all! There were many activities such as horseshoe throw, videogame arcade, imaginary room, and way, way, way more!

Finally, it was the day. Wizards had been eavesdropping, so they set up magic shows and wand shops. While all this fun was happening, one wizard was in disguise! This creature was actually a leprechaun! You know that leprechauns love gold and jewellery? Well, this leprechaun was a very greedy one! Every single thing that could shine in the sunlight attracted him! He eavesdropped on Elsanna who announced it. He heard that it would include a lot of jewellery! When he entered, he was scandalously amazed! Before he could do anything, he took out his bag and started running from shop to shop, stuffing jewellery in his bag and finally was about to exit when he realized someone was casting a spell so that he couldn't move!

He looked around to see who did it. It was Elsanna who cast the spell with her horn! She had a frown on her face, and all the other wizards and unicorns, alicorns and pegasusses were pointing their horns or wands directly at the leprechaun. With a trembling lip, he blurted out why he wanted to steal all the jewellery, and he said his apology. All the creatures looked at each other and looked back at him. Without saying another word, all the creatures apologized back. But before anything else happened, there was a BOOM and a CRASH, and all the creatures looked up to see what had caused all that sound. Their eyes grew wide; they saw that a dragon was causing this trouble! With a blast of magic, though, the dragon fell down dead.

THE END

Candy Land

Have you ever wondered what Candy Land looks like? Let me tell you how this place looks. Candy Land is a magical place full of children's dreams. Whenever a dream comes true, candy makes more kids' dreams come true!

Here are some creatures who live in Candy Land. A cloud critter lives in the sky. This is a real animal that has a job to make every kid on earth be unique and special. Another creature is a sparkle siren. These mermaids and mermen are covered in sequins and sparkles. Their job is to raise the sun and to raise the moon. Each year, they pick a place and live there for a week. This year, they chose to go to outer space to meet some friendly aliens. The president of Candy Land has to choose people he thinks have the ability to go to outer space and find some alien friends.

News spread about the trip to space. People chose to go and be nice to the president of Candy Land so he can choose them, but that never helped. It only made them get fired from their homes and make new ones all by themselves! After three weeks, the president had chosen people who would go to outer space. He demanded all the people to stand in a straight line with straight backs and to remain silent. When it was his turn to speak, he said that whoever is the fastest to go to outer space to meet a friend will come back and be the president of Candy Land.

A great chat of excitement could be heard, and then the president bellowed, "SILENCE!!!" And finally, there was silence.

When it was time for the president to remark to the people who he thought would go to outer space, there were dozens of gasps, and people started to gape at each other. The first person was... drumrolllll... Annabelle Lee, a pretty girl with blond hair and a rainbow headband. The president kissed her on the hand and led her to the first rocket ship. She waited for the rest to accompany her since it was her first time getting chosen by the president. The next person was... drumrolllll... Bluebelle O'Doyle, an ugly but strong looking girl with blue glasses. She skipped to the president, and he patted her on the back. Then she did a backflip to her rocket, grinning from ear to ear. And finally, the last person was... drumrolllll... Alex Li, an old man. He walked calmly to the president who gave him a fist bump of encouragement and then skipped to the last rocket ship. In three... two... one, the rocket ships exploded in the air followed by colourful fireworks.

Alex was very excited. This was one of his most fabulous adventures. If he could be the fastest, he would be the president of Candy Land! How exciting. He shot right up to the sky and was passing clouds faster than an airplane could do. In two minutes, he landed on the moon. No one was in sight but thousands of aliens! He didn't know how lucky he was! So, he got to work by getting out of the rocket ship and saying hello to all the aliens. While he was on the moon, Annabelle was struggling to get her rocket ship out of a tree. Bluebelle was also trying to keep herself from throwing up. She had pressed a button that said "fastest" and the rocket had gotten out of control and was crashing down to the earth at super speed!

That meant that Alex had at least more than one hour to meet an alien and make friends with it. He had made a friend with an alien in no time at all already! He made friends with a friendly alien named Polka, an alien who could calm down fiendish creatures. They talked about themselves and started to like each other.

That day, Polka had bad news! He heard that a flying worm was going after Alex, Bluebell and Annabelle! He told Alex as quickly as he could about it. Alex was astonished. He never knew that. He quickly ran to his rocket ship and took off to Earth. He found Bluebell lying on a tree, trying to jump out of it, with her rocket ship lying on the grass. He took out his lasso and lassoed her to his rocket ship and told her all about it. Now they were heading to Annebelle to tell her about it. They flew to where Annebelle was and found her stuck in a thorn bush, crying, for dear sake!

Alex lassoed her to his rocket ship, too. He told them all about the flying worm. They were so shocked their mouths fell open, and Alex had to close them with a mighty push with a hammer! They flew to Candy Land. They told the president all about it, and he believed them so he got the strongest and most daring knights he had in the land to protect the island. In a few minutes, there was a whoosh and a flying worm landed on the land. The knights gasped and took back when the president wasn't looking. The creature had wings bigger than the castle. His teeth were the size of three bananas together. Its skin was blue with shiny sequins. He could also blow fire hotter than lava! He blew fire until everything was burnt down.

"ATTACK!" cried the president as he ran into the forest.

Suddenly, there was a CLING and a CLANG. The president turned around to see what all the noise was. He was shocked to see that Alex was the one fighting off the worm, using the president's sword! He slashed and banged with all his might that sweat was pouring in his eyes and was dripping into his mouth! Thinking that enough was enough, he made his last move. He ran backward, did a backflip, and punched the worm in the eye! The worm howled in pain and flew away in fear.

Everyone cheered for dear life! They hugged Alex more than googol times! Finally, the president made his way through the crowd and crushed Alex with a loving hug. When the president was done hugging everyone, he made an announcement. It was... that day, he was giving up his job and letting Alex be president! He was so s-h-o-c-k-e-d, he was peach to green to grey! He was as stiff as a stone and as speechless as a bug. Then he broke out in a happy scream. And for now, Alex's dream was to protect Candy Land!

THE END

The Kidnapped Ones

A family full of dragons have some funny names:

Spots
Stripes
Boxer
Miranda
Blue-fire-bell
Brains
Rehcroco

They live in a very dark and creepy church. Whenever you take a step, you make a big, loud CREAKING noise. All the doors creak when they are opened, and the food all has fifty peppers in it! For work, the dragons have math! For example, this equation: $895 + 987 - 901 = 981$, or times tables. For playtime, they set everything on fire and see who does it the fastest! And now, they want revenge, so they decide to kidnap someone! They are going to kidnap a gigantic werewolf named Grey-fern. She is a female!

She has five pups named:

Electric (their baby brother)
Fuzz (their big brother)
Sunflower (their big sister)
Lotus (their baby)
Snowy (their other big big sister)

The dragons decide to kidnap all of Grey-fern's pups to murder and eat. She lives behind a waterfall with her friend Snowflake. She is a slimy white creature that has red laser eyes. Her arms and legs can stretch longer than you, Elaine's and my dad's body all combined together. They start their journey by flying to the cave full of amethysts and sapphires. When they get there, they see amethysts and sapphires everywhere! They decide to empty the bag of rubies they get and fill it with sapphires and amethysts until... there is a BOOM, BOOM, BOOM, BOOM, BOOM, BOOM. Then silence. Then there is a BAM, BAM, BAM, BAM, BAM, BAM and silence. Then finally, all the dragons turn to Captain Underpants! Then to Trollala; then Ashton teaching Mia how to ride a chicken upside-down backwards! They know who is changing them! Grey-fern is! They know that she has magical powers to make things transform into other things just by thinking about them for two minutes and then by forgetting them.

Meanwhile this was happening: Grey-fern is set to escape because she knows she would never let her little kids be kidnaped so she goes to the hardest-ever-to-find hiding spot. She is going to hide in a whale's belly! Of course, she would not leave Snowflake behind so she decides to bring her along. They sneak to the island of suffering swamps. There they spy a lot of dark magic creatures. The first creature they see is called magic skulls! They go into an evil witch's house! But how do they get inside? They sing a poem and the last creature has to say a magic word to make a magic door to appear so they can walk right through it and then to open it!

The words they sing are these:

we sing with pride to the dark side,
none to decline our pride
no way to be lying
or else you will be dying!

They followed these creatures and were stuck in a band of the evil witch's army!

There were:

Seven Chokers who can make you choke with all their smoke
Ten Hailers who make their enemies wail
Six Rooters who are experts at crushing
people with their roots
Eight Stinkers can make you turn pink with their super stink
Four Fork squads can poke and jab

And so many more! They follow these creatures into a castle. As they do, suddenly, one hailer, spotting them, starts screaming orders to the other creatures to get all their friends and start fighting Grey-fern and Snowflake with dangerous weapons. Snowflake helps Grey-fern to fight. She uses her laser eyes to burn the weapons to ashes! While Snowflake is fighting, Grey-fern starts to fight too. She lets the weapons right away fall in her mouth, so she can munch on them.

Finally, they give up and let the army bring them to AntiScorcher! She returns to her evil personality and is finishing off five more prey! This is what she does. She gives a list of things for the enemy, and the enemy must repeat what she just said! If she gets one word wrong, she will make her turn into a wand for one of her witch students since she is the headmistress of the School of Darkness! If she gets the list correct, she will turn her into a frog and make her one of her frog servants. Sometimes, she does that and sometimes she may trap you in a circle of burning hot black fire!

Grey-fern has a great memory. So does Snowflake.

As Snowflake prepares their kids and starts to think hard, this is what she says, "Give me a smoothie with mud, fish scales, aunt urine, camel spit, and five flies on the very top. Then draw me a bath of mud. Make my bed out of poison ivy, bring my slippers to me at sunset and prepare a snack for my scorpion."

It is good Grey-fern remembers what she had said, so now they are poor servants. All the dragons sign-up. Sitting in the cave, they try to guess where Grey-fern is. Well, not every single werewolf is doing so. Sunflower isn't because she's a nice werewolf, born to be nice to other werewolves and bring harmony and peace to the werewolf world. Suddenly, it hits her. She stands up and starts yelling reasons they shouldn't kidnap Grey-fern's babies. It is no use! They can be friends with her instead! So, they travel to places that are farthest they could think they could find her. They first fly to AntiScorcher's castle and find her with Snowflake, lying on the floor exhausted from work. When they see them lie right beside them, they freeze. There is silence for a long time until the dragons break the silence and apologize. Once Grey-fern accepts their apologies, they live terrified of AntiScorcer ever after.

THE END

Are You Ready, Freddy?

Long ago, there lived a big, scary black witch named Onion Stench. She lived in a poisonous river. BEWARE of this river because it causes a lot of harm if you ever disturb it.

This is a list of things it may do to you:

If you touch it, you will grow red wings
and purple chicken pox.
When you swim in it, you become an ugly, big, green shark
If you drink some of it, you become a
blue and pink polka-dotted pig

So now you know why that river is so h-a-r-m-f-u-l! Guess what? Onion Stench wasn't alone at that lake. Under its surface, she had a big gang of great white sharks to protect her (Oh my gosh!). She used these animals to protect her from her enemies! She lived near a screaming ghost named Abracadabra!

Abracadabra lived in Ghost Town where
you can meet a lot of ghost friends:

Berlin
Laisy
Weeze
Candy-mouth
Jacky-pot
Sugar-Slum

And way more! Berlin was Abracadabra's brother. Laisy was their pal. Weeze was their enemy. Candy-mouth was Berlin's and Abracadabra's mother. Jacky-pot was their other bully and Sugar-slum was the bully's mother.

Every single day, Abracadabra and Berlin went to a Monster Fun Fair to meet some monsters and see their talents. When they chose a few talented monsters, they would bring them to Ghost Town and set up a show for the other ghosts who lived at Ghost Town. The ghosts had to pay for a ticket every time they wanted to go see a show. A show cost $200 and including tax, it would be $200.25. There were five judges to pick who was the best and most talented of all, and then they would give a special prize to that monster. It would always be different so you would never know what it would be each time.

Abracadabra kept a list of things she
thought the prizes would be:

A big cup of yellow ice cream
A big blue and purple kit of art supplies
A pink Bugatti
Six red robot servants
Rainbow shoes that sprout wings and let you fly

A small named Slumper ran the Monster Fun Fair.

He was very clever because he could:

Sing and dance with all his might
Put a puppy on a kite
Name a feeling with a second grin
Then he jumps and dances again!

He may sound just like a frantic pig, but he was no chicken. He was more like a trophy! On every Saturday and Wednesday night, the shows started, and they usually lasted five hours.

In this Monster Fun Fair, there was a fun arcade where there lived a boy who was very lonely! The only friends he had were the ghosts who never wanted to show this boy to the monsters because they knew monsters would run and eat him with one gulp (how terrifying!).

One day Onion Stench was staring at her globe. But it wasn't just a globe. It showed you anything you wanted to know! You just had to stare into it and ask the question that you wanted to know. The ingredients for how to make this globe included a bag of rubies and a massive real rain cloud! Onion Stench was working on a challenge. She was heading south and capturing the little lonely boy named Leo! The thing she wanted from him was a ruby from her globe! He had one of them so that was why her magic globe wasn't working well. Leo knew this because the ghosts had told him all about it! So, Leo's goal was to go south as far as possible to get away from Onion Stench.

These were a few big places he could go hide in:

New York
Russia
China
Italy
United States
United Kingdom
France
Columbia

It was hard for Leo, but that was the only thing he could do, so he picked New York where he could hide in museums and other secret places where a stranger or a kidnapper wouldn't find him. When Leo started on his way to New York and was reaching in his backpack to get a drink, out popped Abracadabra with a sunny smile on her face.

Then she sang, "I'd never let go of you, Leo. I just wanted to come along with you."

While they were walking, Leo was silent and was thinking so hard that he became scatter-brained and suddenly instead of looking forward, he was looking back and tripped on a stone. When he got up, Abracadabra was nowhere to be seen, at least until he was going to lean on a big tree when all of a sudden... BOO!!! Abracadabra was there right behind Leo the whole time until she figured out that he didn't know where she went!

Still walking, they finally reached New York and were already close to a shop that blended well with the houses, so they decided to go there. When they got in, they realized that it wasn't a shop! It was a one-house hotel! They saw that there were marble halls and golden and soft beds, sun bursts, satin curtains, crystal lights and more old-fashioned stuff. For the food, there were chocolate Rice Krispies and mango juice! Leo definitely was ready to live here, so he unpacked his stuff and started eating his pasta that was packed in his backpack. Once he was done, he got to work to make things look untouched, so when Onion Stench entered the hotel, he would be nicely hidden under his bed and no one would find him. After twelve weeks of living there, he decided to go and do some speedy shopping. He first went to Dollarama to buy some fancy wallpaper and some glue to decorate the hotel.

Then he went to Walmart to buy:

Apple cider
Oranges
Apples
Rice Krispies squares
Strawberry jam
White bread

That all was very cheap, so he bought two more items that were a bit more expensive: a T-shirt and shorts. When he got back, he realized that Onion Stench was already in New York! He had to hide under his bed immediately. When Onion Stench entered, she noticed that someone used to be living there because Leo had forgotten his groceries. When she busted into Leo's bedroom (where he was hiding), he could smell onion! The smell was so strong that it made him sneeze! ATCHOO!!! When Onion Stench heard this, she turned around to face the other bed. When she did this, Leo leapt out, slapped her butt and then was piggyback riding her! YIPPEE YEEHAW!!! Leo was having so much fun, he tickled her neck! When he did, a sprinkle of happy magic controlled her. When he finally got off, Onion Stench was now a kind witch! So, they lived together like little fairies spreading magic everywhere.

THE END

Ice Cream Sundae World

If one day, I went outside and all of the grass and trees had turned into an ice cream sundae world, I would start the day by eating breakfast. I would go outside and lick all the trees and the grass until I was full of ice cream sundaes. After I was done eating my breakfast, I would go to the forest and explore all the places I can find that are interesting. When I came back from exploring, I would be very exhausted, so I would decide to go back home and get a cool glass of ice tea. After I finished with the ice tea, I would feel like watching a movie in the basement all by myself, and since I have a humongous list of movies, I would choose a very interesting and loving one. I would watch Boss Baby or Tangled! Watching and watching, after staring at a screen for three whole hours, I guess I would go call my friend and ask her if she could go and take a hike with me. I would love to go and see the sun set, so I would pick a mountain that takes ten hours to make it to the top, so when it was time to go back home, I could see the sun setting and the northern lights!

It would be fun to do that, so that day, I would wake up early and get to work. I would drive to a very far place and get all the tickets I needed to get so that I could go on the hike. Sooner and sooner, it would be closer and closer until... TICK! It would be time for the hike, so I would walk outside to join my friend! VROOM VROOM VROOM VROOM! I would be driving the car to the hike, so I could get there quicker than her.

When my friend arrived, I would see that she was wearing a lot of winter clothes when it was actually summer, so I would ask my friend, "Why are you wearing such hot clothes when it's summer?"

She would explain a very interesting story all about why she was wearing such hot clothes. This was her story: She declared that she lived in a very hot and creepy place. The next morning when she was walking to the stream to take a sip of cool clean water, she slipped and landed on her bottom. She yelled and looked at the floor as if she had walked on ice, and saw that the floor was in fact iced all over. She tried to break it, but all it did was make the ice on the lake freeze even more. She stopped smashing and went back home. She walked outside once more again (s-l-o-w-l-y), and she said that she was carrying a gigantic, heavy axe. She dragged it to the ice, and with all the strength in her body, she lifted it and SMASH! She yelled, but it wasn't a smash. It was a CRASH! She was heavy in her real weight. She was heavy, but guess what? Since she had the weight of the axe, she was doubly as heavy as a whole whale shark! The whole story just meant that since other places were getting very cold, and since my friend fell in a lake that was freezing cold, and it was very deep, and she didn't want to catch a cold by staying in the cold water, she decided to wear warm clothing. Also, since she didn't watch how the weather was going to be on the hike, she brought warm clothing, hot clothing, and cool clothing.

Since she needed to carry all the clothing, I had to wait up with her, so she wouldn't get lost! I spent the whole time listening to the story instead of walking up the mountain, but it still was an ecstatic experience listening to such an excellent, amazing, marvellous, adventurous, and silly story. I hurried to go home because my tummy was hurting, and I had skipped lunch! When I got back home, I opened the door, ran inside, and washed my hands to get ready to eat. Once I finished my meal, I wondered how the trees and the grass would be like the next morning!

THE END

Imaginary Friend

I once had an imaginary friend named Selena. She was also a very flexible child with blond hair, violet eyes, and a little nose shaped like her mother's! I loved her because she was always very kind, funny, adorable, and very small. She was also a very interesting girl because she explored all the time. Her favourite things to do were to eat scrumptious treats, try to talk with animals she met, and make new things that helped her to be more productive than usual. Her best friends were me, Ashton, and Sophie.

Ashton is my cartoon teacher that helps me with typing interesting and creative types of stories. His last name is O'Doyle. Sophie, my friend at school, is very clever, chatty, and mindful. Selena was eight years old, and Sophie is eight years old too. I am seven years old, and Ashton is one hundred years old! My birthday is February 21th. Sophie's birthday is January 7th, and last but not least, Selena's birthday is on June 8th. The Great and Amazing Ashton's birthday is October 24th. I at least have 207 best friends who are at school, in classes, among neighbours, and a lot more! For example, a few of my best friends' names are Arianna, Riley, Liyanna, Annie, Christopher, Katelin, Marcus, Annebelle, Annabella, Emily, Rena, Amanda, Eric, Stephanie, Rosalie, Sailor, Isabelle, and more!

Selena loves animals. Her favourite one is a small panda as big as a little box that is the size of a pot of ice cream covered in rainbow sprinkles! Do you have an imaginary friend? Do you want an imaginary friend?

Ding dong ding dong! It was the doorbell ringing. Someone was outside my door, so I galloped to the door and guess who was there! It was a little seal that was trying to get into the house. Selena looked at the seal and carefully carried it to our tank, filled it with cold water, and put the seal into the tank. Now I had a bunch of pets at home: my cat, my dog, my guinea pig, my fish, and last but not least, the seal.

ZZZZZZZzzzzzzzzzzzzzzzZZZZZZZZZZzzzzzzzz! I was at home on my bed sleeping when all in a second there was a RRRRRRRRRRRRIIIIIIIIIIIINNNNNNNNNNGGGGGGGGGG! I got up and saw that the alarm was on, so I turned it off. I was in the middle of another snooze when I remembered that I had to go to get the animals that I got yesterday, so I ran out of my bed and headed to my tank. When I got to my tank, I noticed that the seal was not in it, so I decided to go and run everywhere it might have been. I was so worried about what might have happened to the seal, that I settled down and went to start an adventure to go find him.

Ten hours later, I started to lose hope, so I decided to go back home and keep sleeping. When I got back home, I ran to my bed, covered my face with my pillow, and started to cry into my pillow. A few minutes later, I felt a tiny tap on my shoulder. I looked up to see who was doing it. It was the seal! The seal was tapping me on the shoulder, but he was invisible! That meant that my imaginary friend loves her!

THE END

Invite

If I got a letter from Hogwarts inviting me to the school, I would go because I love magic! If I were going, I would pretend to be Hermione Granger. I would show my skills and make everyone amazed... especially Ron Weasley! I would hear the whisper of the Sorting Hat just like Harry Potter. I would want to be in Gryffindor, just like Harry Potter, Hermione Granger, and Ron Weasley. If I were in Slytherin though, I'd meet Draco Malfoy, Snape, and Tom Riddle. If I were in Hufflepuff, I would meet Lavender and Luna Lovegood. Last but not least, if I weren't in these houses, I would be in Ravenclaw! My favourite professor would be Professor McGonagall because she isn't as strict as Professor Snape. I know some spells, so I would want to learn more about them, so get ready to be amazed by magic!

The first spell I know is called Leviosa. This spell can make someone float. Another of my favourite spells can make an animal turn to a goblet. You use it by calling out this: 1, 2, 3, Vera Verto. One of my most favourite spells is a charm which is used for battles and stuff. You say it out loud like this: Expecto Patronum. This spell can keep away dementors that suck people's souls. Another of my favourite spells is very funny. You say it like this: Riddikulus. This spell contains a lot of positive thinking. This spell can prank other people. It can be silly, distracting, scary and very enthusiastic. It is so hard for me to choose my favourite spell from a group of them I know.

All these spells were taught by Professor Dumbledore, Professor Snape, Professor McGonagall, and Professor Slughorn. These were the people who were the ones in the movie *Harry Potter* who taught him magic lessons and who helped him to learn how to defeat Tom Riddle or Voldemort. I think that Harry Potter is very brave for trying and trying to defeat the dark side. My favourite spell will be a spell of protection.

Love, kindness, and intelligence, that's what makes a perfect magic student, just like me!

THE END

Crushing Trollala

I was totally stuck in a very stinky cave, but the most ridiculous thing of all was that I was trapped in there with a famous troll named Trollala who had a crush on me.

I told her not to kiss me since I was a boy, not a troll, and she said, "Alright, I will listen to you, my darling."

And to my surprise my older sister Matilda pushed me toward the troll, and the troll... KISSED ME! So meanwhile, my sister and I started a big, bigger—in fact, the biggest—conversation I had in my whole life. When finally, Trollala broke into the conversation and pulled my sister away from me and toward her. In a blink of two eyes, I saw that Trollala was struggling to make me dance with her, but I pushed away, so she burst into tears thinking that I hated her. So I checked in my pocket to see if there was anything in it. If there was, I would give it to her, so she could stop blowing her nose in my T-shirt or could stop drying her tears in my hair. Well, this was what was in my pocket: a bouquet of roses. So I quickly put the bouquet of roses right beside her, and presto! In a minute, Trollala stopped crying, and I got squished by a million troll hugs but was saved by my sister Matilda!

THE END

My Pet Guinea Pig

"Mommy, please pretty please, may I have just a little guinea pig because I was wishing to have a small pet like a guinea pig, and I promise to take care of it because guinea pigs are also small, so small they can fit right in my hand."

"Fine, I will get you a guinea pig, BlueBell, and there's the BEST PET EVER CONTEST to train animals and to see how talented your pets can be, and the prize is a pot of pet treats for the pet and thirty bowls of ice cream!"

Since I love ice cream, I'm looking forward to it. I'm crossing my fingers for my guinea pig to win, so wish me luck! After waiting three weeks for my guinea pig, there was a knock on the door, and I knew my pet was being delivered. I opened the door and saw a small package that was wrapped in golden ribbons. The wrapper was covered in pictures of cute guinea pigs. I knew once I opened the box, I would have to train my guinea pig as hard as I could, so I could win the prizes for the contest. I named her Susan.

The contest was two days away, so I didn't have much time to train, so I made a schedule of things I needed to do, and in no time, the day of the contest arrived. It was the middle of the day on a Monday. I started my schedule, which said that on Monday, the guinea pig will have to learn how to climb a rock, how to walk and run, and last but not least, how to slide down a slide and skate on ice, which is the hardest thing for a guinea pig to do.

But since I couldn't waste any time, I started with the hardest thing to do. I went out to the backyard and saw that it was finally snowing, so I could smooth the snow, and the next day it would turn to ice. I looked away from the snow and then saw that the snow had already turned to ice. But before I taught the guinea pig how to skate, I taught it the basic things we had to do on our schedule.

So as the days passed, I could tell that the guinea pig was working as hard as she could, so I always rewarded her. I was so excited that I couldn't think of anything but winning the BEST PET EVER CONTEST.

Today would be the day I got my guinea pig a bow ribbon. I went in the car with Susan, and off we went to the contest. I was surprised that the contest wasn't very far. I arrived and saw that the contest had already started and that everyone was waiting for me because I was to be the first one to introduce my pet. I talked about how much I wanted to get a guinea pig, and after everyone was done, I closed my eyes, hoping it was me. To my surprise, I heard this: "BLUEBELL WITH THE GUINEA PIG WINS!!!!!!!!!!!!!!!!!!!!!!!!!!!!!!!!!"

THE END

Part 2: Stories by Elaine

Chapter 1:

Evie

There was a creature, and it was the most mysterious creature in the land. Stories told about it by the elderly have terrified children, yet strangely, not all children. There was one who was delighted! Have I forgotten to tell you that they were the people of Iraqindrue, pronounced "er-ack-in-drew"? Her name was Evie, and every day, she would see a brown shape swooping through the skies. It looked as if it came from a bird, with gliding, outstretched wings. She told this to everyone, along with the thought that it was the mysterious creature. They mocked her, saying she was crazy. Desperate, she hurried to her grandmother's house. The pair were bold, outgoing, and of course, dreamy. As soon as Evie told her grandma about it, the old woman hurried to her room and returned with a book.

Whispering softly and quickly, she said, "I think you are right. I once travelled to a different place, where I saw the same animal, swooping through the leaves. We will go to that place, come back with evidence, and share it with our country."

Evie was delighted. She ran around the house, gathering materials.

The two stepped out the door, and were enjoying the fresh air when Evie said, "Wait. How do we get there?"

Evie looked at the old woman who looked back at her with dark sparkling eyes.

"Dragon."

The word echoed in Evie's mind. Yes! She thought. She could use Twist the dragon. The journey there was long, and it was hard. Twist the dragon wasn't fit for flying. His wingspan was too short, and his wings were twisted. That had happened from an encounter with a giant.

Now, back to the journey. The first two hours barely got them anywhere. The whole length of the journey was 211 kilometres. That is a lot! And on Twist, one day moved them sixteen kilometres. Evie was fog-brained from flying.

She suggested, "Let's go to the beach! There we can rest a little."

Grandma agreed. Grandma rested while Evie collected seashells. One was pink, sparkly, and beautiful. This she held to her ear and heard a voice, not a sound.

"Give this to Twist, your dragon," was all it said.

She did so, and with grandma listening, Twist said, "I know a witch who is both kind and mean, 114 kilometres away from here. She will help you travel eighty-one kilometres if you are her slave for a week."

Next thing the group knew, they were in the witch's lair.

The witch, in a high-pitched voice, asked, "What do you need? I will do it only if you be my slave for a week."

Dumbstruck, Evie and the others nodded. The witch sent them to work. It was true that she was kind, for she gave them easy, little chores such as washing dishes, cleaning wands, cooking food, and so on. A week was over quickly, and sixteen more kilometres remained until they reached their destination. Twist carried them upon his back for a day, and then they arrived. A beautiful rainforest stood before them. Evie wouldn't go in easily. It was dark, and the rainforest was wild!

Evie stepped slowly, hoping not to wake up any animal. They kept walking, and walking. At dawn, they finally found food. A few ripe banana trees, five stinky durian ones, ten mangos, one date, and a lot of breadfruit. Close to the breadfruit, there were about fifteen honeycombs. Evie was in front and went behind to show her grandma it.

Grandma walked to a fallen tree branch and said, "We will feast!"

She picked up the branch and made a fire. Fortunately, the place was moist, so there were no wildfires anywhere. Every dish was prepared, and a feast was made.

They set out again, only to see a river in their way. The Mississippi. The forest around them had cattail plants, and the trees were dense with long and strong bark, and on the ground was sharp flint and steel. Evie had an idea!

"Why don't we build a raft? We saved fourteen and a half honeycombs, so we can use them as glue, leaves as a sail, bark as a raft, rocks for axes, and cattails for pillows, blankets, baskets, and more! Let's do that. Please!"

Grandma said Evie was very smart and went to work. Grandma would take control of the cattails and cutting trees, while Evie did the gluing and building. When they just needed to make a sail, grandma spotted another brown shape. The two watched in astonishment and the shape circled closer. Evie gasped. It had a white head, yellow beak, and a brown, outstretched body.

Narrator's note: And now, the country of Iraq is named after Iraqindrue. Iraq has a plentiful amount of eagles, and every year, the people stage this story as a public drama.

Chapter 2:

Evie, her grandma, and Twist go down the Mississippi River, get an eagle pet and invent glass.

They finished up the sail and set out on their journey, and the journey was harder than the pair thought it would be. First, they had to defeat the rocking waves that swung them around. Losing their paddle, they decided to go on without it. Crying out, Evie saw that the wind had almost blown away Twist who thrust out his claws, and Evie held them. The wind blew Evie and the others to shore. Surprised, they looked around. They were back in their homeland!

"We went in one big circle!" said grandma.

They went to the very same beach to relax when Evie suddenly perked up.

"We could sell magazines about our journey," she said. "And honey! With the money, we can buy an eagle and relax for the rest of our lives."

Grandma thought it was a brilliant idea and went to her house for some paper, pencils, and erasers. She came back disappointed. Everything was missing! Then Twist suddenly remembered the witch and thought she had some money to buy the supplies they needed. They grabbed their bikes and zoomed to the place. When they got there, they were disappointed to find that the witch was in a grumpy mood.

"Get out of my house!" she screamed. "Did you hear me? GET OUT OF MY HOUSE!!!"

Twist backed up. The others did so too. They quickly turned around and hurried home. There, they had a quiet and serious conversation. They had nothing to do, so they walked around town. Grandma spotted a sign that said "WE'RE HIRING! $200 a day! Our website is HomesenseEllisplis.com" Grandma wanted to join. The others did too. At the end of the week, they had $140,000. That was enough to get an eagle. They did and named her Calf who got her name because she was as dangerous as a baby cow (a calf) which was very harmless. They loved their fledgling, their eaglet, and would occasionally bring her to their lucky beach, letting her hunt in the water.

One day, a volcano erupted, spewing lava everywhere and boiling the water in the sea. The team watched in terror. After a few hours, the lava cooled, except for one spot where the sand was still boiling hot. When it finally cooled, it was a smooth, transparent substance. They put it in their "holes" which were actually windows. They were now cool in their house, and the glaring sun couldn't hit them with its blinding light. Everyone in town was jealous and would pretend to clean the windows while actually trying to steal them. Their plan was unsuccessful—the team kept an eye on them. To and fro, they went in a circuit. Finally, when Twist could get out of the bathroom, he came back to finish his story, or so everyone hoped. Alas, he never left the bathroom!

THE END

The Passionate Passion's Passion

Chapter 1:

A Strange Dismissal

There once lived a young girl named Passion, so named because of her love for everything. She was thirteen years old, and she had a dad and a mom, a little brother named DeDe, and a little sister named Rozie. Passion was in grade eight. Duh! Her siblings didn't even have school. Obviously they didn't because they were only three years old!

Anyways, right now Passion was at music class, the last subject before dismissal. Her teacher, Ms. Marionette, was still giving her boring lectures about famous musicians. Passion already knew most of them: Wolfgang Mozart, Ludwig van Beethoven, Michael Jackson, and the Beatles! She also knew some songs from this bunch.

Ms. Marionette then said, "And I wish you a good weekend; time to pack up!"

Passion sighed with relief. She could finally go home! She got up from the carpet. Her backend (tailbone) felt like hot iron. She took a few steps toward the front door.

"Passion."

Slowly, Passion turned on her heel. It was Ms. Marionette who had spoken. Passion froze. Her relieved and comfortable feeling was gone. She gulped down a wave of fear.

Ms. Marionette said, "Come."

Passion reluctantly obeyed, following Ms. Marionette out of the classroom, down the winding hall, past the principal's office, and into a maze of turns she had never entered. She thought, I am going to be late for piano class. Ms. Marionette stopped abruptly and Passion crashed into her. Passion startled out of her thoughts, and mused, well, let's see if Ms. Marionette knows her way through this maze. Ms. Marionette led her through the corridors. Finally, they stopped. She looked at her Fitbit. Somehow, it was still 1 p.m. the time they ended school. Ms. Marionette opened her mouth and spoke a prophecy.

"One born of a dragon, bearing darkness and light, shall rise to the heavens over the still land. The moon's light eternal, brings a promise to the planet, with bounty and grace."

Passion recognized this prophecy. She shivered. The prophecy repeated in her head, and she didn't remember screaming. She felt it inside and outside as a feeling of no privacy. She blocked her ears to keep it out. Finally, when she had calmed down and made sense of what happened, she already felt overwhelmed and her knees were shaking. She also caught a glimpse of Ms. Marionette's face morphing into a kraken's. She had no time to register it in her brain, for she felt a clawed hand at her back pushing her. She almost fell onto the stony ground, but suddenly the world seemed to spin around, and she was in her yard. No time had passed, and Ms. Marionette was nowhere to be seen.

"Passion!" her mother's sunny voice spewed from the backyard door, and she felt a cold floating presence around her.

She heard a cry from DeDe, and Roza whined. Passion had a thought that they were probably eating lunch. This spread a warm sensation over her, and the cold floating presence disappeared.

She smiled and replied, "Yes, mother?"

Her mother, starting a conversation, said, "I need you to come inside! It's 1:10! You also have to get dressed because you're going to piano soon! Before though, tell me about your school day!"

Passion sighed, knowing that she had to yell because the babies continued wailing. She had the same routine as always: telling her mother about her school day, getting new diapers for her siblings (yuck!), and washing clothes, having piano class, and finally, brushing up and going to bed. While she slept, she had a nightmare.

Ms. Marionette was now a dragon, repeating, "You will pay."

On the 211, she lunged and Passion screamed. Her window opened, and in came her... best friend!

"Amy!" she cried in surprise. "How did you get here?"

Tossing a streak of her beautiful blond hair down her shoulder, Amy's face turned to a horrible twisted one; her eyes were red and her hands were claws. And she attacked. Passion woke up. It was daytime, 8:00 a.m. according to her Fitbit. She yawned, got up, and got dressed. She combed her long midnight hair and brushed her teeth. Hurrying downstairs, she poured herself a bowl of cereal. It was Saturday, so she didn't have school. She secretly winked to herself, ready to start a new day!

THE END

Chapter 2:

Again and Over

As soon as Passion managed to get past breakfast, she went right away to her favourite chore: cleaning the attic. Most of her classmates thought it was boring and dusty, but Passion's perspective was different. She thought it was pretty fun because she got to find old prized possessions there, like a nice treasure chest full of books, a signed copy of *Huckleberry Finn*, old gardener gloves, and countless other things! Well, she kept a collection of these possessions she found in the attic. Her collection was very big—a whole bookshelf of objects! It was her most prized possession. Back to cleaning the attic. She grabbed her favourite brush and shovel and started upstairs.

"Passion!" her mother's sunny voice was drifting up the staircase. "What are you up to now?"

"To clean the attic!" cried Passion breathlessly, for she had just finished going up the stairs.

"Ta glon tha atti," mimicked DeDe who was three and a half now.

He had just learned how to speak words, and was now using them for good practice. Passion just ignored that and walked into the attic.

In the corner of her eye, she spotted a mysterious box. Walking over, she wondered what was in it. She opened the lid... and there were a bunch of straws and strings of a variety of colours, and a perfect teal pair of scissors. She right away went to work, knowing exactly what to do with her lucky find. In two minutes, the attic was cleaned. She brought the box and its materials downstairs.

As soon as she got down, she took the scissors and cut a winding piece of red string. She also took two straws and arranged then in a X shape, tying them together. She took the red string and weaved it around the X until it was a huge rectangle of red. Slipping out the straws, she made a perfect huge quilt! She then gently placed the red quilt over her siblings, who were now asleep. Just then, a bell rang. She had to get ready for swimming class! Looking at her Fitbit, she saw 11:30 a.m. She had swim class at 12:00 p.m. so she had better get changed.

Just then, her mother called, "Passion! Swim class! And don't make me remind you again!"

"I know!" groaned Passion who was tired of being reminded.

Just then, the babies started crying. They had woken up and just discovered the quilt they were under. Ugh, thought Passion, they ruined it!!!

But, just then, Passion's mother called again, "And change... NOW!"

With a big sigh, Passion got changed.

"Mother!" she called. "I'm ready!"

Passion's mother lumbered up from the basement. "Yes, fine, I will drive you," she said.

Passion sat in the car, waiting impatiently because it was now 11:39 a.m. and she might be late for class because of the heavy traffic. Her mother was just sitting there, not honking her car horn. Just then, the traffic light turned green. Her mother didn't pay attention and didn't move the car. Passion got upset.

"Mother, please get the car to move!"

Passion's mother put her foot on the gas and crashed into the car in front of her. Passion screamed, the seatbelt snapped, the door flew open, and she was flying out of the car. She landed hard on the road, her left leg in searing pain. She also had a major cut on her torso. She tried to get up, but she was surprised to discover that she couldn't do so because her wrist kept bending and twisting, and her other arm could not support her, because when she moved it, it exploded in pain. The ambulance came and took Passion on the stretcher. Her mother sat up. She was in the middle of the road. All around, citizens were crowding around. Passion's mother felt a surge of anger at Passion and started blaming her for the crash.

"Passion did it! It wasn't my fault! That's why I'm unharmed!"

These words flew out of her mother's cruel mouth. Then, she heard sirens. She, turning around, saw police approaching.

She started, "Passion did it because she—"

A policewoman touched her shoulder. "I heard that, now come with me. We need to talk."

In the hospital, Passion started getting back into shape even though she still had a broken leg, an arm in a cast, and a twisted wrist. Just then, a nurse came in. She had a name tag with "Sophie" appearing on it.

Sophie said, "Passion, a friend is here to visit you. Her name is Amy."

Passion's heart jumped. She remembered the night when Amy lunged at her. She tried to remember what happened before, but all she could think of was "again and over." She heard footsteps. Through the door came Amy.

Sympathetically, she said, "I brought you a couple of lollipops. I'm allowed to stay with you for a couple of days. I'm so sorry about the car crash. I am also sad to be the one to tell you that your mother has Alzheimer's. She was diagnosed yesterday. That means you will be living with me for the rest of your life."

Confused, Passion asked, "What's Alzheimer's?"

Full of grief, Amy replied, "It's a deadly disease that shrinks the person's brain. There is no cure for it. That's why you have to live with me or else live with a neighbour or simply be an orphan."

Passion inquired, "What are they doing with my mother?"

Sadly, Amy replied that as a matter of fact, they were taking her to the gallows to be executed because Alzheimer's was very contagious.

"I'm really sad that your mom has to go there," finished Amy.

She handed Passion a cherry lollipop. Passion undid the wrapper and licked it, loving the tangy taste and then put it on the nightstand, saving it for later. Pulling out a candy cane to put in Passion's drawer, Amy clambered onto the bed. Passion could hear her hospital gown crackling. Amy hesitated, slid off, and reaching into her suitcase, she pulled out a signed copy of *Peter Pan*. Clambering back onto the bed, Amy opened the book. Deep into thought, Passion read.

After two hours or so, Passion stopped, out of breath. Passion looked around for a bookmark, finding the candy cane and hooking it in. Her stomach growled. Just then, the hospital lunch bell rang.

"Great!" cried Amy. "I started to think I would starve to death!"

Passion laughed, used to her little jokes. They hurried out of the room, walked into the lunch line, and set down their food on the table. Taking a sandwich, Passion took a bite. It was delicious. Ham and cheese, maybe. Amy took a gulp of her chocolate milk.

"Why, you've got to taste this!" she cried.

Passion took the straw, jabbed it in the small aluminium circle. She, too, took a sip. She nearly gagged when the taste sunk in. It was WAY too chocolatey.

"Well, this is the best!" Passion choked with fake enthusiasm and forced a smile. She quickly devoured another bite of her sandwich. Just then, the sound of beach music sounded in her ears.

"What's that?" Amy asked when Passion rose.

Passion absently replied that it was the dessert bell. Amy jumped up. Passion didn't flinch because she was used to Amy's love of sweets. Well, maybe she was also brave!

THE END

Selene's First Lesson

There used to be a little dragon named Selene, who had red scales, a yellow belly, and an arrow-tipped red tail and who could also breathe out ice instead of fire. A timid dragon, Selene was always staying in the shadows while others took the spotlight.

Her parents thought that it was time for her to take the spotlight, and so they signed her up to be in an orchestra.

Selene nervously sat in the car, wishing she could be at home.

Then her mother announced, "We're here! And get ready, don't be nervous!"

Selene, having exited the car and entered the studio, stumbled inside the classroom crowded with a lot of dragons.

Professor Draco announced, "Everyone, one by one, you will go onto the stage and introduce yourself. You will say your first and last name, your favourite colour, your birthday, your age, your favourite hobby, and where you live. Then you will say something special about you. I will say your number. Parents, please return to your vehicles."

Almost everybody filed out, until there was only a quarter of what there used to be. Selene heard her name called first. When she made her way to the front, a kind, bearded dragon gave Selene a microphone and told her to introduce herself.

She said, "Hello, my name is Selene. My favourite flower is an orchid, and orchid is my favourite colour too. My birthday is on April 3ʳᵈ. I am eight years old, my favourite hobby is knitting and I play the violin too. I come from DragonWaters Creek. I'm not a usual dragon... I breathe out not fire, but ice."

Everyone gawked and started talking about her. It was a big, loud mess. Selene tried to sneak to the doors, but she was very, very distinctive so everybody spotted her.

Then the kind, bearded dragon said, "Silence! Hello, Selene! My name is Draco. You may play the violin in the orchestra."

At that very moment, everyone began complaining about how they wanted to play the violin. Draco breathed out fire, and everyone was silent except the ones who were whimpering because they were burned.

Draco whispered to Selene, "Our numbers are what we call each other; for example, you are Number Seven, and when you raise your hand to go to the washroom, I will say, 'Number Seven?' and you will say, 'Washroom!' That's how we communicate with each other."

Draco said, "Number One!"

A pink dragon with a heart-shaped tail and purple belly said, "My name is Violet Reline. My favourite colour is purple, my birthday is on September 7th. I am eight years old, my favourite hobby is crafting, and I also live at DragonWaters Creek. I don't breathe out fire—I also breath out ice."

Violet, who was actually next to Selene said, "If you are smart, answer this riddle. A book has 500 pages. The first page says that exactly one page in this book is false. The second page says that exactly two pages in this book are false, and so on. The 500th page says that exactly 500 pages in this book are false. If one page is right, which page holds the right information?"

Selene replied, "The 499th page."

Without hesitation, Violet commented, "I didn't expect that! How do you know the answer?"

Just then, the bell rang. Selene walked away, trotting through the doors.

"Selene!" It was Selene's mother, calling from the car.

As she got out of the car, she asked, "Did you make any friends?"

Confidently, Selene replied, "Yeah, and she sits right next to me. Her name is Violet, and she also lives at DragonWaters Creek. Can you make a playdate for us? Pretty please? With some ice on top?"

Selene's mother smiled. "Sure, but only if you know the address and play in the orchestra!"

Selene replied, "Yes, mama! I will!"

Selene's mother winked. She got in the car.

"Come on!" she said.

The two rode home.

THE END

The Prince's Dragon

There once was a grand castle. This castle had big problems. There was an old, greedy king, and a kind, young queen. This king told everyone to pay him gigantic taxes for simple products, such as a box of rotten strawberries which would cost $30, 009, 345, 395, 832, 091, 728. In this case, no one dared to buy anything. The queen kept trying to convince him to lower the tax. But, no, the king refused. Days passed. The king still said no. One day, the queen bore a son. He had brown hair, green eyes, small hands, and a special crescent-shaped birthmark upon his forehead.

He grew up to be everything the palace wanted him to be. He was brave, loyal, and true. One morning, the prince awoke to screams. He quickly changed, washed up, and ran downstairs. The royal entrance burst open. And there stood a tiny dragon, the size of his head.

The prince said, "What was everybody screaming for?"

The prime minister replied, "This dragon was from the Elein Age."

The prince didn't need to hear more. He knew the Elein age was when dragons roamed the land and destroyed it.

Breathlessly, he said, "Leave this matter to me. Stand guard like you did before." He hurried to his bedroom and said to the dragon, "I'm going to make you a home. Stay safe, okay?"

The dragon answered with a timid squeak. He put the dragon in a cardboard box. The box burst into flames.

The prince said, "Control your fire! You might put this castle in flames."

He put the dragon in his mother's pet cage. The tiny dragon clawed his way out. The prince tried to put him in the closet, but the little dragon clawed at the prince's hand until the prince took him out again. The prince tried the garage, the mailbox, the grand meeting room, and other hilarious ideas until the prince gave up.

"Ok, just live with me!" said the prince.

THE END

Lonely Joey

Once there lived a lonely boy in a land that was at war. His name was Joey Meyer and he always begged his mother to get a friend. On his birthday, he wished for a friend. Suddenly, with a flash of light, Joey was facing... a bunch of stones!

"Hey!" Joey yelled. "I didn't ask for any stones! I want a friend!"

The stones disappeared, and there appeared a small little girl about his age who wore a little frilly pink dress; a girl whose eyes were blue and whose hair was black. She stared at Joey with an interest that gave him the creeps.

"H-h-hello-? M-my n-name i-is E-Elena," she stuttered.

"Hi!" Joey said. "Will you be my friend?"

The girl simply nodded. Joey tried teaching her a game of chopsticks, but she kept asking questions! Joey finally managed to teach her hopscotch. She was an amazing hopper—she drew a very long hopscotch that ended on thirty and jumped the whole game with ease, finally managing to tell him about her.

Her birthday was August 1st—she was twelve years old. Her birth stone an emerald, her favourite colour green, her mother was... Isabelle Meyer! That was Joey's mother, so they were twins! But they both had bad thinking and didn't realize it. And that meant that he had more than a friend! He explained this to her in a few minutes, and then he asked her where he was.

She said, with a sly smile on her face, "Home, brother! Follow me to Monster Hollow!"

After a bunch of turns leading to everywhere imaginary, they were at WOMB! The World of Make Believe.

Joey stared at the entrance. It was a... rat!!! He stared at it. It was tiny, and it was NOT a door!

Elena said, "Start!"

And the rat said, "Which is the one with a pure heart?"

Joey stepped up and said, "Me!"

The rat said, "Pass a test!" And then it turned into a raccoon, saying, "If I change form, do I still have the same heart?"

"Yes!" cried Joey.

The rat turned into an old door, opening creakily. And staring at them, in the doorway, was a monster. It was more terrible than he thought.

It had a:

Dragon's eye
Platypus' beak
Ram's horns
Devil's spikes
Shark's teeth
Snake's tongue
Horse's mane
Giraffe's neck
Crab's claws
Octopus' legs
Bird's tail

And lastly of all, the monster bore the sign of peace upon his forehead! That meant he was on the good side! And that meant he was their companion!

THE END

The Wishing Spell

Boom! Ruby woke up, got dressed quickly, jumped out the window, got caught on a zipline, and after the zipline ride, she got past a stack of lollipops when suddenly she dropped onto the porch of her tree house (you may think it's almost the end, but it's just starting!). Ruby always went to her tree house. But one day, when Ruby got to her tree house, Ruby accidentally fell in a pool, and a whirlpool formed.

Blast! Ruby was in an imaginary world!

There was a note beside her that read:

THE WISHING SPELL

To make a wish, find a potion bottle. After you have the potion bottle, put it under a full moon for two days. Take a locket that binds together two loved ones. Melt the locket and put the locket in the bottle. After that, take a piece of lunar rock. Mash the lunar rock to powder and pour the powder inside the bottle along with the liquid and light and do it quickly so the locket won't turn back into a locket. Drink the mixture and don't complain. Think of your wish, and it will work.

The note was long although Ruby didn't waste a second. She went to work. First, Ruby tried to find a bottle, looking everywhere, including on the grass and gravel. Then she remembered what her mother had said.

"Only the cleverest will find out."

Suddenly, Ruby noticed that her pocket was bulging, and inside was a big bottle! Although she did not know she would get help from friends, she started with herself.

She tried to get to the other side of the world where everyone was asleep, not needing to worry because in a second, a gigantic crane landed in front of her and asked, "Other side of the imaginary world? Hop on!"

So, she did, and in a moment, they were at her destination! It was a full moon! Happy, she jumped off the crane as soon as it touched the ground. She set the bottle on the ground. As soon as it touched the ground, it started shining. After two minutes, the shining stopped! It was ready.

So, she set off to find a locket that binds together two loved ones. She went underwater and was surprised that she could breathe. She tried to find two mermaids, and suddenly she met up with the mermaid queen and king. They could read minds, so the king gave Ruby a locket! He told her to go to the Flaming Pit where the kind witch Charcoal lived.

"Thank you!" said Ruby. "But I need transportation!"

So, she borrowed a seal and shot off. In one hour, she was at the Flaming Pit. Charcoal was there, greeting her. She quickly melted the locket and then poured it in the bottle.

She gave Ruby a magic globe and said, "Ask this globe a question. The globe will answer."

And suddenly, everything disappeared, and she was back on land. She asked where to find a lunar rock.

"You are standing on it right now!" replied a sweet voice.

So, she picked up a rock and crushed it to powder with her globe. After that, she poured the powder inside her bottle, barely controlling her excitement. She drank the whole bottle and thought, I want to go home! And she was home, at her tree house, but she wanted to go back to that world, so she purposely stepped in the pool and smiled as a whirl of colours began to swirl.

THE END

Fendy and the Esurient T-Rex!

There once lived a very adventurous little dinosaur who always looked on the bright side. She was very brave too. She even protected her sick mother from a ravenous, malnourished, and totally esurient T-Rex! Her name was Fendy!

One day, Fendy had to start school!

"Can't you homeschool me? Please? Pretty please? With a meatball on top?" Fendy begged her dino-mother.

"Sorry, Fendy, but I can't homeschool you because once you're signed in—you can't sign out unless you're expelled!!!!!!!! And don't try to get yourself expelled because it wastes my meatballs!!!" her mother replied.

So, Fendy asked, "Can I go to school online?"

"Yes! Of course!" her mother replied.

So, Fendy whooped with joy and went upstairs to her beloved playing room. That was where she kept her beloved clay sets. She loved them with all her heart, but that doesn't mean that she didn't love her mother with all her heart too. Although she had made a complicated bowl of fruits yesterday, that didn't mean she wasn't going to model today.

She was going to make... three little, golden clay monkeys! One had its hands over its ears, one had its hands over its eyes, and the last one had its hands over its mouth. Fendy also made two little imaginary friends, Matthew and Flora. She also kept a little pet dragon that was green because green was her favourite colour!

Then her mother called, "Fendy, time for dinner!!! You have chicken, beef, and steak again! They are your favourite foods!"

Fendy's stomach rumbled. She realized that she was hungry, so she hurried downstairs to the living room. She hurriedly ate her dinner, but the meat was spicy, so she had to drink a lot of water. After that, she quickly wrote one page of her supposed-to-be-two-page journal. That was her only homework from home, so it was just plain work to her. She got to play in the playroom or watch a movie after work. In her mind, she bet that there were a lot of bullies in the school, and even online they would tease and insult her. She was different from others. She had rainbow braces (which none of the other dinosaurs had, as they didn't need braces), a special claw mark from the esurient T-Rex she had battled, (none of the other dinosaurs had defended anyone, as they were really busy), and she was a small chatterbox and a bit too outgoing. But that didn't bother her. She loved being unique and different. But she was afraid of heights and hated fast vehicles, especially being in them. She never went to Disney or Disney World because she was afraid of roller coasters. But she wanted cotton candy—she was a sugar bug!

She was afraid the teachers would make her introduce herself and the bullies would tease her. So, she watched Mary Poppings, a special way of saying *Mary Poppins*. That distracted her from bad thoughts about school. She felt more optimistic and didn't worry about small things. She just fixed them. It was hard, but worth it.

When it was time to sleep, she got nightmares about being black while the others were white, and it wasn't a school; it was a whipping place. The teacher was whipping her, and she bolted upright, and ate a small candy chocolate that had started melting under her pillow. Then, she felt better and fell asleep. She dreamed of Candy Land this time, and that was good!!!

THE END

79

A Living Statue, A Living Shadow, and the Half Animal Forest

Two good friends, a living statue and a living shadow, had been friends since they were babies. However, one day, they both had to move away. One moved to a desert while the other moved to a lost island. When they were separated, a hurricane blew though both of the places they had moved to; one hurricane was on a lost island while the other was in the desert. Meanwhile, very nice weather prevailed in the place they were born. Their parents wanted to go back there, and they agreed. So, they went, and they reunited with a joyful greeting!

One day, they went outside to go exploring, and they stayed outside forever because they couldn't find their way home. Instead, they bumped into a half-flamingo half-puffin which looked pretty weird because it was a pink puffin with a long neck.

"I know this place! This is the half animal forest! It's a little scary but it's the best place... ever!!!" the shadow cried.

They spied a half-rooster half-iguana, half-pig half-donkey, half-crab half-sheep, half dolphin half horse, half-dragon half-rabbit, half-leprechaun half-elephant, half-dog half-cat, half-bat half-salmon, and stag! They passed a half-mole half-Greywolf, half-panda half-turtle, half-butterfly half-tiger, half-frog half-crocodile, half-killer whale half-ladybug, half-zebra half-eel, half-sturgeon half-lizard, half-ape half-kangaroo, and half-centipede half-ostrich. They were so busy looking behind them, that they did not notice that they had walked straight into a half-twenty headed snake half-twenty headed spider's web. That is one scary animal! They tried to free themselves, but it did not work. Suddenly, half-Greywolf half-mole were surrounding them so quickly that they couldn't escape. A genie suddenly appeared, and they wished to be back home, and with a WHOOSH, they were back home. THE HALF-END!!!

THE END

Harry Lunettes

Once, there lived Harry Lunettes, a boy who liked to dream. He attended Cold Spring Harbour, the biggest and best school in the world! But before you get too happy, Tom Catcherclaw, the school bully, also attended Cold Spring Harbour. Mrs. Lia, their teacher, was a kind but strict teacher. She watched Tom on exams because she didn't want to see him cheating!

One day, Harry was bullied badly. When school was done, he walked away, not caring if he was going homeward. He ended up lost in the woods! And then, he bumped into Leo, a very lonely boy.

"Hi, Leo," said Harry without looking up.

They knew each other because they were friends!

Leo said, "Do you want to meet Charcoal, my mother?"

Hearing this, Harry immediately cheered up!

"YES!!!" he cried.

Charcoal was a powerful black witch but a kind one. They went to Leo's house, and Charcoal was on the porch waiting for them.

"I've been waiting for you," Charcoal said. She opened the door and invited them inside. "Welcome to my home."

She gave them some vanilla smoothies and they also ate some carrots.

"Charcoal likes to steal from the selfish rich," Leo whispered to Harry.

Next, Charcoal led them to the jewellery room which was filled with jewellery and gold.

"Can you add something to my collection?" Charcoal asked.

Because Charcoal was so kind to Harry, he gave her a golden amulet that was in his pocket.

"You found it!" Charcoal cried.

"What do you mean?" Harry asked her.

She explained that she had been looking all over the place for it. She let Harry live with her because she knew Harry's family was mean to him. She also gave Harry phosphorescent slime and got rid of Tom (I guess you forgot about him!). She punished Tom by making him stay in a poisonous river and then stay in a polar bear's den where he was eaten. They also made a robot!

THE END

Sapphirstine & Amethystine

There once were two sisters named Sapphirstine and Amethystine who had a truly remarkable grandfather! Sapphirstine's favourite colour was any shade of turquoise, her eyes were sapphire blue, and her heart was full of trust! Amethystine's favourite colour was any shade of violet, her eyes were amethyst purple, and her heart was full of confidence and courage! Their grandfather had a sister named Isabel who was a blind beggar!

One day, their grandfather, whose name was Ricky, went outside to check for the newspaper! He was surprised to see a particular bunch of keys on the doorstep! He picked them up and went back inside. He was surprised to see that the room was empty! He looked upstairs, downstairs, and in the basement. No sign of his granddaughters. Just then, when he was about to give up, he went out to the yard, and there was Ricky's family, having a picnic and talking!

He said, "Isabel, I'm back!"

Isabel quickly motioned for Sapphirstine and Amethystine to come to Ricky. They obeyed, and he showed them the keys.

"Where did you get these?" asked Amethystine.

"Found them," he muttered.

He ran all the way to a mysterious lighthouse, turned the keys, the keys clicked, and he opened the door. There, a headmaster was waiting inside. That's Arkiba, my old friend! Ricky thought.

Arkiba opened his mouth and said, "I will make you very, very happy and wealthy!" and then he disappeared.

Ricky went back home, and it was night time; plus, it was Christmas Eve! They saw that, for their presents, they'd received a bag of rubies and the crown jewels! They also received grinning snowmen to help them cheat on exams and on other very hard things and then they had a very delicious dinner. They weren't overjoyed because Arkiba was gone. They searched for him, but he was just nowhere to be found.

THE END

Chill

Long ago, we Thundermen from Mars, came to Earth with our pets, a tribe of Northerners! Our leader was the oldest woman on Mars! One morning, when we were at breakfast, we were so busy eating that we didn't notice that our leader was missing. Where could she be? Still sleeping? Perhaps not because she always wakes up at 3:00 a.m. to make breakfast, and then she wakes up the Thundermen, who are:

Aricky
Lightning
Dash
Strike
Bolt
Blaze
Coal
Chalky
Sparks
Loyett

Once we finished eating, we finally noticed that our leader was missing! First, we gasped in shock, and then we waited for something to happen. Suddenly, a bottle with a message in it appeared in front of us, and I opened it! All it had on it was prints, bones, biscuits, and toys made from stuff you find in the Arctic!

We called for our pets, "Olly! Strike! Ashyl! Unki! Elite! Really! Azulejo! Bark! Defy!"

Immediately they came, following Azulejo.

We tossed them the message, and Ashyl, Elite and Defy barked, "Bit bays bat bour beader bis bin be brison!"

I hurried to the prison cell and unlocked the door and guess what! Our leader wasn't there! And then another message with a bottle appeared, and the writing was from Isabella, our leader!

You may use the bottle as a drinking bottle, but I'm being kept in enemy territory, and the person who took me was Chill the Abominable Snowman! You must find a way to kill him! P.S. Have fun! You can kill him by melting him!

That's when it stopped, and Chill appeared, and I pulled out a lasso and I lassoed him. But then he disappeared! It was just an illusion to confuse us into wasting time when it was actually time to start making a big, good booby trap!

I immediately made a beige map with a white Chill and grey prison cell and a magenta tunnel leading to a dark dungeon with a light, secret panel to a red, orange and yellow 100% HOT land of fire! Chill rolled downstairs, and time whizzed by. Chill came, we lassoed him, put him in the prison cell, watched the tunnel, moved to the damp dungeon, watched him escape and go through the secret panel.

"HOT!" echoed from the dungeon.

But Chill was gone! YAY!!! He was only a puddle of water now. Isabella appeared, and we had a big celebration!

THE END

Painting the Future

There was an artist who painted the future. He had a son whose name was Gong Grumpy. One day, the artist didn't feel like painting the future, so he decided to make a small painting for Daisy Gong, his real, magical, and wonderful friend, which he would then turn into a real world.

First, he thought of a cat, but he didn't paint a cat because it was too boring. He suddenly got an idea! Ding! He would paint a picture of a hall of mirrors, and at the end, there would be a glowing mirror. It would be ROYBETH RAINBOW! He fetched the biggest paper he had and painted the vision he had in his mind.

"Daisy!" he called. "Daisy!"

Immediately, a shower of sprinkles arrived and Daisy, who always appeared as a fairy, flitted into the open window.

"Hello!" she cooed softly.

"Hi!" he greeted her.

"Be quiet! Please!" Daisy suddenly said, her little voice alarmed.

The artist looked around. There he stood, Gong Grumpy.

"Playing with your little puppet fairy friend?" he asked meanly.

"I'm not a puppet!" Daisy cried.

"It's okay," the artist finally managed to say.

By the next hour, the artist was already asleep. When he got up, the fairy was gone and so was Gong Grumpy. Then a cry for help came.

"HELP!"

He swivelled around and saw a giant snake chasing Daisy!

When Daisy finally looked at the artist, she flew over to him and said, "I accidentally turned Gong into a snake."

He smiled at her. "That's good!"

"Why?" Daisy asked, confused.

He smiled and gestured toward the painting. They were so busy talking that they didn't see the snake slithering up behind them.

He said, "Because then Gong won't follow us into the painting."

Daisy was much more cheerful by now, so she opened the painting, and they walked to it! When the artist stepped in it, he was pushed back by a sudden force. Daisy saw and was concerned, so she tried also, but she was pushed back.

THE END

The Twins In Hikueru

Two twins, named Yvonne and Elaine, were very close. One day, they went to the library to read about warnings in fairy tales when the librarian tossed them a book about real warnings. They read it. And guess what! They finished it the day they got it although it was five inches thick! (that is fast!) And when it was time for lunch and dinner, they did not talk (their normal habit is to talk their heads off) because they were thinking about how the first warning was their favourite warning. Oh, and by the way, their dad is the richest man in the world. That is rich! The next morning, they woke up at the same time: early before dawn. They talked about their plan to steal $7,000 from their dad while brushing their teeth. GURGLE BLA BLOOK BLA. They sneaked into their dad's room after changing and guess what! Instead of seeing him, knitting and talking to himself, there stood a dwarf. The twins were so shocked that they immediately took out their listing notebooks and charm pencils and started listing these characteristics about the dwarf, who:

looked like an elf
was wearing a red and yellow scarf although
it was the middle of summer
looked like Pimplestinkin because I think he is
was wearing a primrose and aqua sweater with buttons
was wearing rainbow pants
had violet glasses
was bald with a little bit of hair that was grey

When they were done writing, the dwarf looked up at both of them.

"I've been expecting you two," he said.

He reached in his pocket and took out a name tag. It said "Pimplestinkin" in blue writing.

He said, "My name is Pimplestinkin. I will help and be with you in your adventure."

Yvonne and Elaine blurted out, "We're not having an adventure! We never had one."

Pimplestinkin looked offended. "If you never had one then you are going to start one now." He reached in his pocket again and took out a time bomb. "Look deep into it and imagine outer space," Pimplestinkin said.

Then, everything disappeared and they were in outer space.

"Look for the special box," Pimplestinkin said. "It will take you to Hikueru, the lost island where I used to live."

"What does the special box look like?" they asked Pimplestinkin.

He answered, "It looks like a treasure chest."

Elaine, Yvonne and Pimplestinkin searched until Elaine cried out, "I think I found it!"

The others hurried to Elaine and she gave them a special box. Pimplestinkin took it from her and opened it.

"There's a note inside it," he noticed. "It says people who have received the letter must go to the lost island Hikueru, and find the diamond eye." There it showed a picture of a diamond. Pimplestinkin continued, "But BEWARE! There is a mysterious snake pit hidden there." He stopped.

He took out the time bomb again and his serious expression told them to look deeply into the time bomb and imagine Hikueru, the lost island. Everything started to disappear. And then the twins were in Hikueru. They gasped in wonder as they gazed around them. It was Hikueru, but no! Hikueru was A-M-A-Z-I-N-G and A-W-E-S-O-M-E.

"Come on. Don't just sit there watching," Pimplestinkin said.

His voice interrupted their thoughts. They got up and started walking. Soon, they had travelled a mile and suddenly they fell into the snake pit. They scrambled to the diamond eye while the snakes got confused and ate each other until they were gone. But one remained, slivering toward them.

Pimplestinkin yelled, "Watch out!" but they didn't hear.

Only Yvonne saw, and she told Elaine, but suddenly jumped out of the pit to avoid the snake. Elaine quickly grabbed the diamond eye and killed the snake in the eye by stabbing it with the sharp tip of the diamond. Suddenly, in a whoosh, they were back home. Their mother asked them if we wanted spaghetti, and they nodded.

THE END

Rosalina the Baby Snow Leopard

If I had a memorable dream, it would be a dream from a long time ago when I was three! In it, I was exploring my house, but in a second there was a... BOOM, CRASH, BAM, THUMP, RAT TA TAT TA, BOO, and I followed the noise. I followed the sound until I found out that I wasn't at home anymore. I was in a mysterious forest, all by myself. Not a single animal moved! All of a sudden, leopards leaped and blocked me in front, so I moved backwards, but a gang of wolves blocked me in the back, followed by lions that blocked me on the right, followed by a bunch of black panthers blocking me on the left. I was surrounded by my most terribly scary dream animals that I had heard were all blood-thirsty—which was the feeling I was right now having. So, I decided to take a seat (in the muddy dirt!) and I counted sheep until I was at number three thousand, two hundred and ninety-nine! After three hours of sitting down and waiting, all of the animals from the safari jungle fell asleep so I slowly tiptoed out of the sleepy head group.

Walking and walking. It was so boring to keep walking and never stopping to check the map (I didn't even have a map to check). After five minutes of walking, ten minutes of walking, fifteen minutes of walking, twenty minutes of walking and so on—RRRRRRRRRRRR! I heard a very impressive ROAR that shocked me. How could a person make such a loud, impressive, musical, adorable, attractive sound? Since I really wanted to learn how to make such an amazing sound, I followed the sound until I saw what was making it. Do you know who was making the sound? I don't either, so let's find out to just keep walking till we find out what is making the sound. Click clack, click clack, I was walking and following the sound while walking. Closer and closer, I heard the sound get louder and louder for me to hear it clearly and more clearly. When I looked at who was making the sound, she growled at me when I looked up at the attractive animal. Guess what it was? It was a little baby snow leopard!

She was also very happy to see someone like me, so she was licking my face all over to let me know that she liked me. So I played with her, she was so cute and happy that she had a great big smile on! I was just wondering what the day was going to be at the end of the day! So, I held the snow leopard and I named her Rosalina and since she liked her new name, she purred, and I looked at her, and she saw my whole face.

The sun was setting, so I decided to go to sleep with her, she snuggled up in my arms, and we went right to sleep. I was awake for a little snack the next morning, and I decided to go to the lake and get some water. I looked up and saw that I was walking down the path, and I saw a tree that had watermelons on it, so I decided to get a small box, and then I decided to go put the watermelons in the box, so I could go carry the watermelons that were in it. Bringing it back to the lake, I petted the snow leopard. I had to go get some snow for it to eat, so she could come and get some watermelons with me, so I could stop being scared to go all by myself! That was the end of my dream.

THE END

Part 3: Essays by Yvonne

Essay 1: School Should Be Free

Have you ever had a favourite subject at school and wanted to know more about it? Or have you ever asked your parents to take a class on your best subject, but once you start yipping with joy, your parents come in to tell you they don't have enough money to pay for that school? Well, if you have had any of these problems, you will agree, we should make education free!

First of all, what's the difference between going to a school that costs money and having school that does not cost money? There's really not much of a difference.

Many poor people can be smart at one subject. Usually, they always want to go to school, but they don't have enough money. We could fix this by making school free! Poor people could learn other new subjects. Once they are very good and win some scholarships, they could use that money to enter competitions. Poor people will try their best at competitions to win it. If they win them, they will get a trophy or a medal. Once poor people get a few trophies, they can sell them and get some money for more food and furniture they need.

Now you can see how making school free makes a big difference from starting to make kids go to school and making poor people wealthier by going to school without paying.

Think about staying home every single day and not going to school. How you learn is by having a lucky old person in your family or one related to you to teach you, if you are lucky. It would be really boring. Homework wouldn't be homework any more. Fun wouldn't be fun anymore and fair is not fair now. That would be really bad for a community and could really worsen the community.

Once all the poor people are gone, mainly all the people in the community are rich, but there would be only a few of them. Having only the people who have money go to school is a form of segregation. The people with no money can't go to school and the people with money can go to school. We can solve this solution by making school free, so all people can go to school, no matter what (well, only if they are not sick).

Now then, you have seen the difference between making school free and expensive, and the reasons that we should make school free.

Essay 2: Cooking

Have your parents ever told you that you should learn to cook? Have you ever heard your parents tell stories of them helping their parents or grandmas and grandpas by cooking at a small age such as eight or nine? Well, it's always true that those stories about your family are role models of sorts, and there is a reason why you should try to achieve it too, and you should learn how to cook! These kids were helping their parents cook!

Right now, you may be thinking that cooking is normal and that usually your parents cook, so why should you care? Actually, you should care because learning how to cook by yourself can help you in the real world. Knowing how to cook could also solve problems such as this one: once all your family members die, you can cook, so you don't need to buy any fast food or any unhealthy food. But there are many reasons you should learn how to cook.

For example, being able to cook could also help you help homeless people. Giving food for free to homeless people is a small but kind way to act.

You should listen to what your parents are saying because being able to cook is a big help to your life. My first reason why you should learn how to cook is that it can help you in the real world. There are always challenges that can block you from your goal which you need to get past. Many people cook because being healthy is a big part of their bodies, and eating healthy foods can help them to exercise well.

We should make cooking classes mandatory because imagine you finished a whole day of work and are very exhausted, but you still know you need to cook a meal for your kids. This would make you even more tired because you would really be making yourself do more work when you have done the most you can do already. A solution to that problem would be to get your children to at least help or cook a meal for themselves. This could help parents get some rest instead of doing all the work. So that is why kids should learn how to cook.

One more reason that kids should learn how to cook is that it can make children start eating instead of being picky. They eat more because when kids help their parents cook, the kids eventually will get very tired. But once they think about how hard their parents worked the whole day and how tired they are and still need to cook a meal, which is now tremendously tiring for them, kids will appreciate their parents for cooking meals for them and show their appreciation by eating more healthy food and not being picky.

Where should cooking be taught? Cooking could be mostly taught at school because usually parents work all day long somewhere else, and if the kids burn down the kitchen, it would be very bad and worse if the parents weren't there to look out for their children. Also, cooking classes at school would have more people which is more secure than at home where there were only two or three people. Cooking at school could also be good because your school knows what allergies you have. At other cooking classes, they don't know your allergies, so they might cook something that you are allergic to, and if you didn't know and ate it, that may be bad for you.

Cooking can also help you do other activities such as crafting or painting. You may be wondering how it makes you better at painting and crafting. Many people who cook usually like to make their own recipes or explore what they can do while cooking. That is the same as painting and crafting. For crafting, you also have all the materials you need, and you also have your freedom. This means you can make whatever you want because there is no wrong or right object to make. Painting is also the same because you can paint what you want to paint, not what others tell you to paint! It's all your choice. Whether you want to blend your colours or not. Whether you want to use watercolour or colour sticks! It is always your choice.

When I say this, it always reminds me of the difference between me and Elaine. My dad says Elaine is a naughty but creative girl. She always likes to follow what she wants to do instead of what the other people tell her to do (even if it's good for her—she still won't do it!). I am quieter and not a chatterbox. I am always doing the things my parents tell me to do, and I like to follow instructions more than creating my own ideas. That is why cooking reminds me of the difference between me and Elaine.

One last reason we should learn how to cook is that cooking is an everyday job. If you know how to cook, you can survive. Without eating, you can't survive. If you have children, you would also have to cook three meals for them each day: breakfast, lunch and dinner. Usually at school, parents make lunches for kids but that will cost some money, and sometimes the food would be something you don't like, or it is a little rotten. Learning how to cook is a must-learn activity to help you live.

Cooking could also be a little fun because you can do whatever you want. From following the instructions to making your own food. Cooking, then, is a big part of your life and learning how to cook will be very useful for you once you grow up.

Essay 3: Anti-Smoking

Have you ever seen people smoking in public? Have your parents told you to stay away from those people? Obviously, your parents should tell you that because smoking in public should be banned as it can be very unhealthy for children and adults.

A few years ago, smoking was discovered to be unhealthy. Many people decades ago would always smoke and would say that, if they smoke, they would feel relief from boredom and exhaustion, but their reasoning really wasn't true.

Smoking is bad for people because it can make it harder to breathe with their lungs. Cigarettes have this sort of bad chemical that can ruin their lungs. In their lungs, there is this tube called a trachea, or you could also call it a windpipe. That's where when you finish chewing food and swallow it down. In the lungs are little tubes called secondary bronchi. The secondary bronchi lead to another tube called a tertiary bronchi. The tertiary bronchi lead to another ball, not a tube this time. This ball is called bronchioles. In a cigarette, there is this chemical called carbon monoxide. This chemical reduces oxygen, which is bad for your lungs. And this can lead to many diseases such as heart disease, artery disease, and more.

Why do people still use cigarettes? People still use them because they think it can cure their exhaustion and boredom, but really, smoking makes them even more tired.

Many smokers also throw their cigarettes on the ground, thinking it is okay to do so because it is just one tiny small object. Smokers shouldn't do that either because cigarettes can actually cause fires if they are thrown onto grass, bark, and many other growing plants. People who smoke should throw their cigarettes into the garbage instead of the ground because forest fires or fires can cause much harm to people and animals and the environment. The fire can burn habitats animals live in which can make the animals move somewhere else, and maybe the other places are already burned down because of the people who are smoking throwing away cigarettes onto the ground. Animals are going to die and suffer from being unable to have any homes to live in because all of their homes are burned down; a crisis whose solution is to plant more trees though many animal habitats take a full year to grow well and new just like the burned ones. So, mainly we could just try to make the smokers stop throwing their cigarettes onto the ground and especially where many animals live and where their homes are and where the fires burn easily.

Lastly, how can we get rid of smoking? We don't need to get rid of smoking. People who are smoking should just stop smoking and eat healthy foods and become more active to make their lungs better and let oxygen go through their lungs nicely, in and out. Smokers could also keep exercising if they are still tired because exercising is always good, and 60% of being fit is being healthy and being able to live longer.

Smoking, then, can be bad, but we can still smoke only a little and try to go outside to exercise more. Smokers should also try not to throw their cigarettes onto plants and cause wildfires or forest fires where animals live. It can ruin their habitat and if all the other habitats they live in are gone, it would be pretty sad. It would be sad for animals to lose their homes, and it would take a long time for the plants to grow again, resembling how they were before the fires. So, I say people should try not to smoke.

Essay 4: Global Warming

What causes global warming, one of our most challenging problems? It doesn't mean that this situation does not have a solution.

Let's start with how global warming is caused. Global warming is caused by different factors, one of which is the gas or fuel produced by vehicles like cars, buses, planes, boats, and trains, and more. When gas or fuel gets released, it will travel to the atmosphere, a thin layer of gas surrounding the Earth to protect it from the hot sun. The fuel that gets released from vehicles usually thins the atmosphere and can cause the temperature to get hotter and seep through the atmosphere and onto the Earth, causing many problems, and not just for polar bears.

What's another cause of global warming? Many wildfires cause global warming because they also release a gas called carbon dioxide. How can we prevent wildfires from spreading? We can prevent them by not making campfires when camping, or if you need to make one, don't use hardwood. Use softwood because it's hard for it to cause forest fires, fires that will burn out once it is midnight or so.

Another way that global warming is made is the waste in landfills. Garbage, causing pollution, starts with landfills that release landfill gas that is mostly made out of methane and carbon dioxide. These are both greenhouse gases. Methane in large amounts is poisonous and explosive.

Now let's talk about the dangers of global warming causing many other problems such as coral reefs that start to bleach. Bleaching means when the coral dies and turns white.

Global warming is when the world heats up the atmosphere, making it thinner, and the sun's heat is seeping into our world, warming it. We call it "global warming" because the world is warming but not just in one area—the whole world is getting warm. That means all the oceans, grasslands, and more.

In the sea, coral bleaches by losing its food. The coral's food is called polyps. They are tiny little animals that the coral eats as it grows. Polyps do not like warm water, so when the sea is getting warm, they leave. Consequently, the coral is without food and dies as it bleaches.

To conclude, I will suggest that everyone should always make wise choices so as not to worsen global warming and that we should never try to refuse to change the world but to reduce global warming, so no animals and people will face the harmful challenges that it presents.

Essay 5: Masks

Should we make wearing a mask mandatory? Everyone should agree on the answer, "yes." Think of the number of people who have died from coronavirus. Think of the number of people suffering from the loss of a family member or friend who has died of this sickness. Can we prevent this sickness from spreading, and how can we get all the people to participate in our methods of prevention?

First, we could fix this problem by getting everyone to wear a mask at all times when they are out, no matter where they are. Our parents should teach us how to wear a mask properly, so no germs can spread. Babies do not need to wear a mask, but they also shouldn't go out to places—a mall, for instance— that have other people. Babies should stay inside because, you know, a baby going around in a tiny mask would look and sound funny.

It is important to wear a mask.:(
Wearing a mask is important.:)
It isn't very nice to stick your tongue out at your sister.
Sticking your tongue out at your sister isn't very nice even if she deserves it.

How do masks work? Masks can protect your mouth from germs that spread through the air if someone coughs or sneezes. A mask can do this by blocking the parts that germs can enter and sicken people. These parts are the mouth, and rarely, the nose. That is why the mask is covering your mouth and your nose completely. When you feel the papery part blocking your mouth and nose, it sort of feels like a coffee filter because coffee filters do not have any holes, and so germs cannot get through the mask, and it can't get to the person's mouth or nose.

Many children don't like wearing a mask because it doesn't feel good, it is very hot and sweaty underneath the mask, they can't breathe easily, and they could make many more complaints about not wanting to wear a mask. To fix this problem, what other actions can we take to make children wear masks? If they don't want to wear a mask because it fogs up their glasses, they could wear the kind of mask that has a black hole. When they breathe, the air will go out of it, and it won't ever fog their glasses again. If these terrible children don't want to wear masks because they look and feel bad, then take another action: go to a store to see if they have any masks, check them, and select a few funny ones, scary ones, or ones that have all kinds of decorations. We can fix children's mask problems by being creative thinkers with unique ideas and let the children stand out all they want, so long as they wear masks and their parents do too.

Some kids are told to wear a mask at school by their parents, but once they enter the school, usually they secretly take it off for the whole time, and when it's time to go home, they will put it back on and pretend they wore it the whole time at school. This doesn't just happen at school; it may also happen at other classes, such as piano class, art class, dance class, and more. Many parents have discovered their children have done this and are willing them to stop doing it. As you know, parents usually don't like to make their children upset or sad, but they can't make their kids wear a mask without making them sad. A solution to this problem could be to be kind and share a few challenges they faced when they were little and show them how they thought of fixing it.

Other problems with masks usually involve children who don't want to wear them. No matter what the problem is, the key to its solution would be to be kind and share what you have similarly experienced. A lot of people have been choosing whether to let their kids go to school for education, or to teach them back home, but they are safe at school. Many people are unsure and follow what other parents are doing. Parents shouldn't be doing this because what if their children don't like to do this? Some kids can miss out on knowledge that they don't know yet, or children may get sick staying at school for too long because they don't want to wear a mask. There really isn't an answer for the question of what the parents should pick—the children should pick because both options are good ideas.

Wearing a mask is important, then, and necessary for children—for everyone—to do every time we go outside where there are people. Wearing a mask will help us save each other and we must do our part.

Essay 6: Three Book Reports

I am going to talk about the book *Counting by 7s* by Holly Goldberg Sloan.

Briefly, this story is about a girl named Willow who is a genius who faces unexpected changes such as when her parents die in a car crash. Or when her counsellor is Dell Duke. But in the end, she basically has some sort of close family with her siblings. Her sister is Mai, and her surly brother is Quang-Ha. Her mother is Dung (she changed her name to Pattie when she found out what it really meant), and her father is Pattie's partner.

I learned in the book that unexpected changes can happen all the time, but also that you don't need to be embarrassed or sad because you are not the only one who has overcome unexpected changes. And everyone who knows about this fact of life would surely be trying to help because no one likes to feel that way. I also learned that at least someone is there for you. No one likes to be left out, which is the same as no one being able to be loved or have a family. So, it would be expected that somebody will help take care of you or just comfort you—for example, your friends. Talking to a trusted teacher could also make things better.

This book I would recommend to everyone because it won a few awards that had been difficult for their authors to attain when writing their books. It is also, simply put, a good book.

You can know if a book is good or bad based on whether it has all the elements of writing in it. For example, my favourite element in writing is the plot. The plot starts when a problem begins to form and characters try to fix it. I also like the part when two or more characters talk to each other. That is called dialogue. All books of course have at least one or two elements of story-telling—conflict, plot, character, dialogue, setting, theme, point of view. Mainly all books by writers or advanced authors have a lot of elements to make them good, and they especially add a lot of expression.

Counting by 7s has a lot of expression which makes the reader feel how the character is feeling. Almost no one likes even to act expressionless because no one is used to it, and it's mainly nothing that anyone even should try.

One last reason that I recommend this book to you is that there are many situations which attract the reader to see what will happen next.

This book could inspire someone, but it only inspired me a little. But while reading other classic books, I started to get inspired and wonder in my future if any activities that happened in the books would happen to me too. It only took two books to inspire me.

The first one is a memoir called *The Boy Who Harnessed the Wind* by William Kamkwamba. Briefly, it is about a boy who creates a windmill by himself with his friends and also faces the odds of food shortages since their village suffered greatly from a loss of food from a long drought. In the end, they had a wonderful harvest, and also the boy made a windmill to increase the light in his house. This story was also based on a true story, so that is why I always wonder if anything that happened in the book would happen to me.

The second book is called *The Secret Keepers* by Trenton Lee Stewart. It is about a boy who found a watch that has the power to make him invisible, but there is also a man who has another watch with a different power. The boy has to try to get the other watch or arrest the man. In the end, the man gets both watches but also gets arrested.

If I was the author of this book, I would make some things different. First of all, I would like the story to be an adventure since who doesn't like to read adventures? Next, I would add more special synonyms for the words the author uses because it made the dramatic events become a little boring. Lastly, I would add a quotation at the very beginning. But this book still won a lot of medals, so I would still say it was pretty good.

Good books should have three parts. The first one is the beginning, the second one is the middle, and the last one is the ending. In the beginning, many authors like to introduce their characters and mainly make a beginning of what is happening. In the middle, they start to create their plot. And some of their characters may be in tricky situations. Lastly, the ending is called the climax. That's when the characters have solved their problem and when the author starts to wrap up their story.

To wrap up my book report, I would conclude by saying that though books sometimes seem boring and while you can never remember all the knowledge they contain, actually books are a big part of our lives.

Essay 7: New Activities

Doing new activities is not scary, but many people think otherwise. We always want to help people become encouraged and learn how to do new activities without any hesitation.

To start from the first step, you should have a friend or a parent beside you, so you won't get hurt while doing the new activity such as swimming, zip lining, bicycling, and more such activities that many people often do. Next, ask all the questions you have that concern you and ensure the answers make you feel a bit more relieved. Then, ask the parent if she or he can demonstrate how to do it properly and maybe just to tell you a few tips that can help a lot! Last, just try it yourself! You never know if you will succeed or not, and if you don't, no worries! Just calm down (and make sure you are not hurt) and try again but ensure you know what you did wrong that time and try to fix it!

Being nervous about learning a new activity can always be scary in the beginning—all people have been scared! Even people who are old still have some fears! But this is not something to laugh at and say, "Who cares if I fear this, I'd rather not fix it. There's still plenty of time!"

Actions that can discourage you from doing a new activity would include bullying or being let down by people. A way to fix this problem is to stay away from the people you don't trust, and if you still get teased, try not to tell them all about what new activities you are doing. One last tip you could use would be to ignore the bully's teasing and pretend you didn't hear or even just walk away. At home, ensure to tell a parent about some other ideas that you are comfortable with. I am just giving you some tips I would use if I experienced this situation. To the people who don't get bothered by others who discourage them but are still scared, let me say that everything should be normal if the new activity is a sport or even if you have never seen people do it and never knew anything about it.

We are human beings who try all we can to be successful and need help from each other and need to explore the outer world. But first, we develop with each other and learn one by one. Just like building a staircase out of Jenga blocks! We start with a low start which is when we start figuring out basic ways of life. Then the staircase gets taller and taller, which is when we start growing up and working together. But once it falls, that means there is a dead end, which basically means that all the knowledge we learned didn't make sense any more. So, we rebuild, helping each other again and being confident that we'll find the answer to, say, each math problem or other question that leads us to the answer.

To end my essay, I will have to admit that doing new activities is not scary at all.

Essay 8: Bullying

Bullying is tricky to detect and stop, and not many people know when a bully is bullying because many people who help a bully can tell lies, pretend to be helping, or even just protect the bully by justifying why the bully was bullying. Bullied kids are not going to schools as much, they aren't playing as much, and they aren't enjoying as much free time. They also are not showing enough courage.

People are always trying to find a way to know whether the bully is bullying or just lying. But many people who still haven't succeeded need help.

How can we help the ones who are bullied to become more courageous and fight back, not in fighting, but in a nonviolent way while speaking the truth? Many people believe that they shouldn't even stand up and fight back. They should just remain calm and find a parent who is nearest and also the one they trust the most and tell them what's troubling them and see if they could speak calmly and try to fix the problem. But how can we get the bullied ones to do this when they are weak and scared? Be a friend. Stand up and speak the truth in front of everyone. Speaking the truth won't feel scary since no one will be laughing at you when you are really in a bullying situation. Not cowering but showing you have the right to fix it, you can and will fix it!

Bullying is a major problem now, but you may not notice it. To explain it, I invite you to consider it as a sort of ecosystem! Think about bullies as being like bears. The bears will eat some rabbits which are the kids getting bullied. Then the rabbits will warn each over and stay home in their warren, the bullied ones' home. The bullied ones will not go to school anymore because they know that the bullies will repeatedly "bearly" them again. That's how an ecosystem works!

Among the reasons that bullying is bad is that it makes the bullied people, like my hypothetical rabbits, quit going to school. It causes too many problems that can lead to worse ones, like the bullied one might start bullying all the people in the class or all your friends. The bullied one who will suffer and not enjoy any school days will stop socializing with friends— basically all this can cause a huge problem!

Bullying has increased a lot this year, but why? No one knows the reason, but let's just fix it. We don't solve a problem by waiting for questioning. We will solve a problem by thinking about and doing what's right, just as I said in the beginning! Some ways we could help would be to be a friend, stand up for each other, cooperate in working hard together, and lastly, play together like lasting friends! Acting like a friend is a real way of stopping bullying! We must stand together to make bullying decrease as much as we can.

Bullying has been a tough problem all these years. But we always try to fix it, so that life can be like how it used to be without it. Bullying can still cause other problems, so we are still cautious. Let me say, to end my essay, that we should mind being bullied and think about the right way to stop it!

Essay 9: Fun Facts

The topic for today is why fun facts are a very convenient way for people to learn, depending on how correct they are and how fun they are since kids never like to learn anything if no fun is included in it! Fun facts are commonly the most convenient way for people to learn, a way that can include a lot of games, fun, and creativity!

First, we need to talk about how fun facts are convenient. According to what I think, fun facts can be convenient in all sorts of different ways! For example, of course they can teach kids fun information super fast since not very many facts don't include fun explanations. Fun facts can introduce kids' minds to different ways of how to get over their weaknesses and help them learn in different ways. Fun facts can include many tips that can help them for many subjects.

Fun facts mainly are the opposite of books, but how? The answer to that question would be that fun facts don't right away give you all the information. Fun facts give you only the main idea you want to learn, but books fill in with details, and some even skip the beginning and right away jump to explaining different important parts and different sections. Fun facts would be a convenient method of learning because, if you were learning something new and you used a book, you would be very confused! But if you read fun facts instead, they would be way easier, and you'd probably remember everything the facts said because fun facts can also give you some tips to remember all the knowledge and because sometimes information can be very overwhelming for you to remember!

Let's compare fun facts against online googling. Typically, fun facts would still be the most convenient, no matter how much googling you do. Many people would agree that fun facts have won the battle, but how? We could try comparing by trying to think of as many points as possible for each team showing which one is the most convenient.

Let's start by naming all the points we have for fun facts.

1. Fun facts are convenient because they just tell us about main ideas.

2. They also convey a lot of information because many authors who write books that include fun facts like to write them in all sorts of ways!

For example, I always like my facts to be true and long, explaining all the details and not leaving out a single word that is important. Just like eating a cupcake! I eat the whole cupcake, not just half of it, so I don't leave a single crumb out. Some people write their facts by just saying the main idea of a topic since that's their way! That would mean they would eat only some or almost all of the cupcake but at least leave a crumbly half or even just eat one bite! I think you already got the point I am explaining, so that would be the end of my essay!

Essay 10: Creative Writing Versus Essay Writing

The topic for today will be why creative writing is better than essay writing.

First of all, who even likes to write essays? It is boring, and many people have to do a lot of research to write essays. Instead, people all around the world love to write about creative topics and make up stories! But many people just wonder: why's that? All people love to write about creative topics, but why?

Among the few reasons is that it can express your imagination! Think about one single person who does not use his or her imagination. It would be a crazy time to experience that!

Another reason would be that many scientists don't know why, but people just say that creative writing feels easier or it just feels normal or comfortable to write creative topics or stories. Even I love to write about stories, to doodle, and to do all sorts of creative activities based on imagination.

A few other reasons would be that it builds confidence, doesn't it? It can express self-control and relaxation, and don't forget it gives a boost of the imagination. It can also make it easier to communicate with others and help you socialize!

Creative writing is important because every day kids experience events that are new to them. They learn new vocabulary and subjects too. Learning and experiencing can make curious minds keep growing—and that is very good to experience. Think about what creative writing can manufacture if you get used to it. It will make hypotheses for worldwide questions every day!

These are mainly the most important reasons why creative writing is better than essay writing, but there are way more reasons that go on and on and on.

Why aren't essays good, though? Many people have many different answers to this question, but it ended up being that everyone thought it was less fun and less comfortable! (Well, that's what I think).

Now, let's think the opposite. Essays are bad because maybe essays just need a lot of research, patience, and many other skills that will never make one feel comfortable. Another reason is this: pretend you have a scale, but instead of measuring how much it weighs, it will say 1% to 100%. 1% percent would mean it had only a tiny bit of creativity, and not many people would be interested in reading the essay. What if the scale showed 100%? That would mean that it could count as a bestseller book, or many people would prefer it as a classic and read it every day. Now, let's compare! Beginning on essays. Imagine you submit the essay you wrote that got an A+ when you handed it to your teacher. If I were experiencing this right now, putting the essay on the scale, for a minimum depending on how many spelling mistakes, creativity, humour, complexity and commas and other writing marks it contained, it would be 43%, and if it were the best essay in the world, it would be 65%. Not very interesting, not much fun, don't you agree?

To brighten your attitude, let's move on to the scale of a creative story. Depending on how bad it is, it would be 52%, and if you were to have the best talent in the world to write the most perfect creative story in the whole wide world, it would be 89%. Woo-hoo! That would prove that creative writing is WAY better than normal essay writing. Now what do you say to prove that? To end my essay (or a knowledgeable creative story), I ask you to think about how fun it could be and start one with me, today.

Essay 11: Famous

The topic for today will be why we should respect the famous people that have led us to a new and better future. Imagine having no one to help us be led toward happiness and freedom. Let's start by naming ten of them and by talking about them.

The first of the top ten best people in the world would be Mahatma Gandhi. No one can replace the "great soul Karamchand Gandhi." He was an icon of non-violence, perseverance, strength and equality. We should be proud that we had Gandhi. He was the man that proved the proverb: "No pain, no gain."

The next most famous person is Nelson Mandela. He has been known as undoubtedly the world's most respected icon and is globally recognized for his personal well-being and honour to human kind.

Another of the most famous people in the top ten would be Martin Luther King Jr. I believe in everything King said, especially convinced by his "I Have A Dream" speech, totally a number one colossal man standing up for African Americans.

Another of my favourites would be Albert Einstein, the smartest scientist in the world to me! Albert Einstein inspired and continues to inspire many people with the idea that science has won the battle since, as all people know, the world has two main subjects over which people battle to decide which one is the best: science and religion. Einstein has almost been the most famous scientist for many years.

Let's move on to the fifth best-known famous person who will be Barack Obama, also known as a president who has helped restore equality, saving Americans from a bad future of more fighting between black people and white people.

Now, let's start talking about famous women. Princess Diana helped the world in many ways. She was not just a pretty face but a princess who also needed to be noble to try all the ways to help make the world better. Princess Diana proved that she was a very noble and kind Princess.

These are a few of the most famous people in the world, but many people are still choosing among them. Mostly the presidents were chosen because they do almost the most important job. Well, except for Donald Trump, who was pretty much the opposite of a president, being selfish and thinking the opposite to Obama on every subject and thinking that Americans are the best and that America should be the only place to rule the whole wide world.

Anyway, why we respect many famous people is because some have led us into a better freedom and richer lives. It wouldn't feel good without anybody helping or trying to make a change in the world. Imagining you were a famous person or just imagine you were one of your most favourite famous people. And imagine how it would feel like if you were treated badly even though you helped the world as best as you could. Now, imagine you as your own normal self and try to put yourself into other famous people's shoes. Imagine how they would feel! Disappointed, sad, or even mad. A few examples of how they'd feel would be dejected, downcast, dismal, depressed, mournful, wistful, gloomy, glum, melancholy and many more words that can break your heart and even make you sick and stay in you for many years. An example would be if you squeeze some toothpaste out, and you try to put it back in. It may be impossible to do!

All these years we have already known the importance of respecting our famous ones, including the ones who have brought us a happier future than we'd have had without them. Anyway, do any of you know how tiring it is to try changing the world? It is more tiring than any other activities you have done in your whole life! So, we should be proud to be supported by famous people, and we should also try to make the world better. Every single one of us. To wrap up my essay, let me say that we should all respect our famous supporters who have made the world a better place!

Essay 12: Zoos

Scared, confused, afraid—these emotions animals can feel when they are removed from their families and put into public spaces for other humans to learn about them. Today, I am going to tell you that it hurts to be taken from your family. It hurts to be alone in a zoo, getting insulted by humans from around the world. People of today are trying to support animals and release a few animals into the wild, but zoos have still become a problem.

Animals are people too. We must treat animals with respect as we do humans. We love them. We use them. We are them. Loving animals doesn't mean trying to make someone proud of doing so. Loving animals means doing it for yourself. It shows respect and makes the world better. All we need is a little urging to tell others how we feel and stand on the side that is right for the animals. We could fix this problem by letting animals free from zoos and from cages. We are together. Bound like a book made from single sheets of paper, and caring for each other.

Freeing animals does not just benefit animals; it also makes you feel free. Freedom is one of the most important actions that show we do believe in letting animals go free from zoos. However, this perspective can also cause a problem. People may want to see an animal up close but don't know where to go to see one up close and to learn from one. To fix this problem, we could catch fewer animals for zoos. Among some other reasons we still should not have many zoos is that animals are supposed to choose whether to be taken to the zoo or to stay with their family in the wild. Another reason is that keeping animals in cages is cruel. Another reason is that zoos are just for human entertainment. Some people might not even think zoos are very amusing. A few other reasons are these: if you want to see animals, just go see one out in the wild! Zoos are a threat to animals.

Today many people have improved on this action, but they could do better. Animals are part of us and part of the whole environment. We stand to protect everyone in this world; we stand to live freely which includes freedom for animals. A little change could change the world! A few examples of how to save animals, not by taking away some zoos, would be these steps we could take:

Whenever you see an animal, just look at it from a good distance and don't bother to touch it if you don't know very much about it. Whenever there is a beehive or any little insect homes, don't destroy them. Try to use a long stick and move to a safe spot that has shelters and some food for this insect.

If you are going to the zoo, be careful and listen to what the zookeeper says you should do when you approach an animal because sometimes animals can have a few defense tricks to harm other predators.

If you are out in the wild, and you see a black bear or a grizzly, don't frighten it or move. Just stand still, and if it approaches you, don't yell or scream. Just pretend to be calm. Wait one or two or more minutes—it will walk away. Probably. Or eat you. Then you can die happily, knowing that you have provided food for an animal.

No matter what animal it is, try to be a friend with it and try helping and doing what zookeepers would do to these animals since animals all have different behaviours. These are all the things you need to know to be a friend and to help animals.

Different types of animals all have different ways to be treated. Take, for example, that great Canadian symbol of strength, the mighty beaver, which always tries to be independent. But beavers like to stick to friends and help build each other's dams—they coined the popular expression "dammit!" The same goes with other animals. So, this means that, whenever you know how to treat a cat, don't ever treat a scorpion the same way or other animals too. Animals depend on each other sometimes too. They may make songs or call to each other, or they may have some special features that many other animals don't have. They don't have to warn their close ones to protect their homes or to hide if there is a colossal predator close by. I will repeat that animals are a part of us and the whole word. We must promise to respect them and to love them.

Animals are supposed to be loved because animals make up our world too. For example, a bird would carry berries to its babies, but while it's on its way back, it may drop a few berries—poo berries—which might start growing into new trees or plants. Sometimes, you don't notice that animals can help the world, but you do when you really observe them in the wild. Animals can also help the world by making endangered animals become back to normal. For example, tigers always eat gazelles, and gazelles are endangered. Tigers can switch to another diet such as other animals or sandwiches or sushi. Or birds or other animals that can keep them in good health. Animals have all the things we have. We have feelings, and so do they. Pet keepers have discovered that all different animals have different feelings, but let's switch to a scientist's perspective, whereby animals don't have feelings. It's just the normal behaviour of a wild animal. So, this question about animals' feelings is still a big mystery. So far, all we know is that animals can have feelings, or they can act in their normal wildlife behaviour. That is why we have zoos, but now, we don't need zoos since we could all go to one zoo based on all the discoveries showing whether animals have feelings or if they just act according to their own personal wild behaviour.

To end my essay, I can simply say that zoos have come to be both a threat and a home to animals. Today, we must stand to protect animals.

Essay 13: Play

Exploring, learning, discovering—these actions you can accomplish while playing. Here's a fun fact: do you know that children can learn while playing? Well, that's true. How this learning process works starts when you understand how objects work just as an engineer would understand them. Next, you basically try to plan with tools necessary for the topic you are working on. Playing on your tools or topic can help you create ideas or hypotheses. In science, you observe, but in learning, almost everything you may use while playing.

An example is the tree of learning. Imagine the trunk as a symbol of yourself fully grown when you understand how the world works. You have already chosen a subject that is your calling. The branches represent your development of the subject you have chosen, and you start gaining more knowledge in interests, learning more than you had when you were little. The leaves indicate you at play as you find out the details about the importance of your subject. And for a detailed example, consider a flower or a fruit on your tree that serves as a memory of this knowledge you have learned.

As another reason we play is that we can chill out—a very good form of exercise to help you get rid of that feeling you have when you get angry or disorganized. Playing is an exercise for cooperating with other kids, no matter if they are big or small. Some other ways that you can learn by playing might be as follows: to relieve stress, improve brain function, stimulate the mind, boost creativity, keep you feeling young and energetic, and enhance relationships and your connection with others.

Play helps you develop and improve social skills, play teaches cooperation with others, and play can heal emotional wounds.

A few of my favourite quotes based on this topic would be these:

"Culture arises and unfolds in and as play"
Johan Huizinga, Dutch historian 1872–1945

"Almost all creativity involves purposely playing"
Abraham Maslow

"Surely do not keep children to their
studies by compulsion but by play"
Plato

My favourite quote is by the author Dorothy Corkille Briggs:

"Every child has an inner timetable for growth, a pattern
unique to him or her. Growth is not steady, forward,
upward progression. It is instead a switchback trail; three
steps forward, two back, one around the bushes, and
a few simply standing, before another forward leap."

Have you ever watched *Mary Poppins*? Well, the meaning of supercalifragilisticexpialidocious is a world of laughter and happiness! And what I will always say will be these words: play is the best medicine.

To wrap up my essay, I will tell you that every word in this essay is all true!

Essay 14: Learning

The topic for today will be why learning new ideas and skills is important. Basically, for this topic we will be talking about why learning is good for you. Have your parents ever told you that you should always try learning something new every day? Do you wonder what that may mean, or think about what your parents are trying to tell you? The reason why they told you this is that learning can hold a big consequence in the end. And it really matters for all the new subjects you have learned when you were younger. For example, another reason your parents told you this would be because education gives you with all the knowledge you need to know to prepare for the real world. Learning new skills and ideas can show you that you are improving, progressing, and moving on to a bright future.

We learn when we are little because when you are a bit older, you have no more chances—you are supposed to see your consequences and move on to a more advanced real outer world. Mainly that means that all the life you get when you are older depends on all the hard work you spend when you are younger. One last of my favourite reasons for insisting that learning is good is that the more you know, the more experience you can have in your future!

Let's talk about what you do while learning. The first thing you will do is increase your habit of learning and decrease your habit of playing. The second thing you do while learning is to avoid boredom: these days, everything is getting more and more boring. Working and finding your strength in learning can get you quickly organized in terms of what you like to learn about. Followed by the last one, learning can support you in knowledge and help you to relax. This advice can get you balanced which can make life somewhat like a piece of cake!

Let's review why we have to learn something new. Doing so can enhance your quality of life. What I used to say was: learning provides you with an escape when you need it, knowledge when you seek it, and a great pastime. We can also learn something new every day so that we can reduce stress caused by our homework. Another way to explain it would be to say that you can gain confidence in everything you do. When we succeed in learning something, we feel better. If you feel stressed doing homework, I'll tell you this: knowledge is power. When you have knowledge, you have the will and heart to achieve a lot of goals and to do a lot of activities. The last reason that learning will help is that it can improve your mental health. Learning also includes achieving goals. Goals can improve your mental life.

To wrap up this essay, I will say that learning something new is incredibly important.

Essay 15: Friendship

The topic for today is how to be a better friend.

Let's start with the basics. First, think about what you would want your friend to be like: kind, funny, fun, respectful, and many other characteristics.

The first step in being a good friend is to be able to be trusted. Who would want to be your friend if you are not trustworthy? They wouldn't even invite you to play with them for a game because they know you will cheat. The importance of being trustworthy means that you have the heart to be good and to be fair.

The second step to be a good friend requires listening to other people other than yourself talking the whole time—that shows you have patience toward your friends.

The next step for being a friend is to notice that person's strengths. Once you know his or her weaknesses, help them face them and overcome them too.

The last step for being a good friend is to be kind and silly, getting their attention in something that opens them up to help them in the real world. To use encouraging words and help them face their fear, their enemy, stand up and help fight for what is right. Tell them they have a voice and not to hide it, and use it to help them become powerful, not letting anyone stop them from doing anything that is right.

The hard part of becoming a friend is getting used to fixing a problem right away if there is one between you and your friend. Why do we? To show we care for them, show we feel sad or can feel shame for making someone sad or disappointed.

How we learn to fix a problem starts with these words, represented as an acronym: S.T.E.P:

S: Say the problem without blame in your mind. Blame means you are accusing someone, reminding others what they did wrong rather than what you did wrong.
T: Think of as many solutions as you can.
E: Explore the consequences of all your solutions since sometimes a solution can end up being pretty terrifying.
P: Pick the best solution. The one that perfectly fixes the problem.

These are the whole steps involved in how to fix a problem.

The last step to being a friend is to be funny! Who would want to be your friend if you are not fun? Some ways you can be funny would be thinking of games, or you can have a great imagination. Imagination can help create mythical games which would be fun for you and your friends to play.

My favourite part of being a friend is never forgetting my friend. Shared experience brings memories to you that help you to keep being nice and help other people get friends. An example would be how me and Sophie are BFFs; it started when we met each other in kindergarten at school. Being friends also means staying with your friend while you make new friends. Sophie and I have been friends for three years! We still are playing together and being best friends.

The most important action you need to do to a friend is this: if you are angry or disappointed, don't spread it to your friend. It can ruin your friendship! Instead, there are two choices that you can choose. The first one is to tell your friend how you're feeling and what happened. The second one is to calm yourself by yourself.

Think about how empty the world would be if everyone lived without friends. Well, having friends is what I call gaining power!

Essay 16: Plants

The topic for today will be why plants are important. Have you ever wondered why having plants is important? You might have asked your parents who say because they make the world look better, but that's not the real answer. The real answer is that plants can help us breathe.

We are lucky we are not fish. Imagine you as a fish. Being a fish would be very hard! Fish have gills which means they breathe through their mouths. That's why fish go up to the air when it's raining. To get some oxygen. Now back to plants. Do you wonder how they can create clean and healthy air for us to breathe in and out? It all starts with the sun that shines into leaves. Then the rain falls. The food that leaves need is sun and water. These elements can make the leaves grow. Another thing the leaves eat is dirty oxygen. Once the leaves are full, they release sugar and clean oxygen just like when you grow an apple tree—the sugar gets released into an apple. That's what makes apples so sweet!

Think about where some of the food and clothing we get come from. They do not just appear right in front of you. An example would be that clothes come from food! It all starts when the farmers grow cotton. People use this cotton to spin it into string. They wash it, add colour to it after choosing what it will be, and then sew it into clothes!

Another example would be that we use dandelions to make medicine. There are many objects that plants can give us. Plants are not just helping us; they are helping the world! When they grow, they spread seeds which can create more plants. This process can create more land in our world.

Also, many animals may live in large plants and trees. Owls, for instance, live in trees even as squirrels live in bushes. We must take care of all the plants we can. Planting more plants can help. Imagine the world without plants. No one would even survive for long since there wouldn't even be enough clean oxygen.

Plants have their own ways of catching food and water. Take, for example, the sundew plant, which has little buds that are like glue. Insects may get interested in this and go on this plant that will get sticky and wait until the bug passes out from exhaustion. Then it will slowly wrap around the insect and eat it. Once it's done, it uncurls, acting just like a Venus flytrap. Similarly, the pitcher plant has a tiny pot filled with pollen into which insects will go and start drinking it, but instead, they will drown. The pitcher plant has a leaf on top of the pit that acts like a lid. Then the plant devours the insect.

Have you ever wondered why plants eat insects? Plants are like us. They need food and water. If they are stuck in the middle of a drought, they can eat insects since insects contain some water! We must try to support plants and ensure that nature exists as we move into the future.

Essay 17: Health

The topic for today, class, will be why staying healthy is important! Let's start with the basics. What makes you healthy? All vegetables and fruits, meat and exercise can keep a body healthy. Being healthy can make people stay good and strong, and keep them from getting sick with diseases. Not just eating right can make you healthy. What you do also counts.

For example, if you watch too much TV, some parents say you can get blind from watching the screen for too long, but actually the real result can be felt when the muscles around your eyes start to hurt. Your parents just say this, so they can persuade you not to look at the screen too long. Staring at the screen can cause eye strain. Other habits that can hurt your eyes include reading in the dark. Reading in the dark doesn't cause blindness either, but does cause your muscles around your eyes to hurt too. Well, it still may be bad to do all of these activities, so be sure to limit how much time you stare at screens and read in low light.

Exercising is good because if you treat your body well and if you exercise well, you will learn how great being healthy can feel. For example, imagine a big car filled with gasoline and it has a well-prepared engine—it could still not be that healthy since it hasn't been driven yet. If you don't try driving it, you would not know if it's good or bad since no one has tried it!

Lastly, eating well is very important. Fruits and vegetables are very good for you. They all benefit you in fantastic ways. For example, fruits can make you look good—your skin and hair, for instance. Meat can make you strong!

There are many consequences for what you eat, what you do, and how you exercise. We must ensure we are healthy. That's the reason why we go to the doctor every year, to ensure we know how we are doing. Now let's talk about some serious problems people have had and still want to avoid. People have had yellow fever, the Black Death, malaria, the coronavirus, the Spanish flu, and many diseases that we do not forget. Many of those fevers and diseases killed many people. Especially the ones who were already sick and old. People continue to study and think about the body and about how to improve our health.

Some famous doctors who have changed the world include Helen Brooke Taussig, a doctor who published a book about the heart which helped many doctors to help people. Another famous person, Edward Jenner, born on May 17th, 1749 in the UK, worked as a physician scientist. Elizabeth Blackwell, also a good doctor, born on February 3rd, 1821 in Bristol, became the first female physician. Daniel Hale Williams was an African American doctor.

Being a doctor can take many years of training and hard work. Consider the difference between becoming a plumber and a dentist. Plumbers fix toilets, which doesn't take much hard work and training at all! But studying and taking classes to become a dentist or doctor are hard. There are many subjects they must learn, such as the name of the teeth and where the tooth belongs.

Depending on the details involved, many other jobs can require hard work. But remember, hard work will always pay off. For example, if you are too lazy to wash your face when you are little, you may get pimples. When you grow up, you can develop a permanently scarred face! That's when your face gets scarred from pimples. It can look very ugly. No one would want that! We always try to take care of ourselves, no matter what. There are many reasons you should do so as well—it all depends on... YOU!

Essay 18: Homeschooling: Good or Bad?

My topic for today will be homeschooling. Imagine you were starting school after a long relaxing vacation. Wishing that the vacation never ended, you ask your parents to homeschool you. Wait a minute! Homeschooling means that you pretend you are at school, but you are really learning at home. This is a rare thing to do. People do this only when diseases spread around, just to keep safe. An example of diseases would be yellow fever or the coronavirus. These days, not many people are homeschooling. Only people who don't have enough money to go to school.

John Holt was the person who started homeschooling. In 1999, 850,000 people started to get inspired by homeschooling (www.homeschoolhistory.com). Then, in 2003, 1,096,000 people started homeschooling. Many people got inspired. Then, in 2007, 1,508,000 people took up homeschooling. Finally, in 2011-2015, 1,770,000 people started homeschooling. And homeschooling is great.

Some reasons we shouldn't homeschool or go to school online would be because when you homeschool you might not learn as fast as when you learn at school. Even though having homeschool is bad, people tried to participate in school online!

One reason you should not go to school online is that, even though you may seem to be looking at the teacher, you may be looking at something else, and no one would know since technology is not totally perfect in terms of allowing us to know where someone's eyes are directed. So just having school online is best.

However, even though having school online is bad, there are some good reasons for it. For example, using technology you can do far more special or complex things than you can at school normally. Also, homeschooling may be a bit good because when you are at school in person you only have a snack and lunch. But when you homeschool, you may eat whenever you want. And, you may eat candy—in many schools, candy is not allowed.

The whole point about homeschooling is to provide school to people who do not have enough money to participate otherwise in school. I believe that only people who do not have enough money to participate in school should homeschool. Even though you don't want to go to school and learn, it's a big choice!

Do you know that in some states, kids learn different things at home than they do at school? There are 2.5 million homeschooled students in grades K-12 in the United States. Homeschooling may include subjects that are rare in school; for example, debating classes and sporting classes. If I were homeschooling, I would mainly like to learn history, biography, biology, sports, musical arts, and learn about famous people who have changed the world. Homeschooling would also inspire me to try to donate and try new things for classes. For example, we could gather all the toys or clothes we don't need and donate them to the poor. Or we could sell things. The money we could get would be donated to the poor.

There are many ways for us to support life in homeschooling and going to school in person. Still, I recommend that people go to school in person instead of homeschooling. But if you would want to see how it's like, go ahead and see how it feels. I wouldn't like it because I don't usually learn as much and as fast at home as I do at school. Also, I get distracted by Elaine but not at school since I am in a different grade than her. Well, even though homeschooling might be bad, you may still try it!

Essay 19: Civil Rights

The topic for today will be civil rights. Have you ever read a book about people refusing to do what the white people say to do? Well, let's imagine that the main section of the book is about black people who, for good reason, often take part in peaceful protests to protect their civil rights. For example, before the 1960s in the United States, if some black people entered a white people's restaurant, most of the white people would want to drive them out. Instead of acting like cowards, some black people sat patiently in their chairs waiting until they got served.

A person who played a role in peaceful protests is Martin Luther King Jr., a black man born on January 15th, 1929. He worked as a Christian minister and died on April 4th, 1968. He also led black Americans to better lives. He showed how everyone had to be fair. His most famous speech is "I Have a Dream." There are way more people who have been participating in peaceful protests because of his influence.

Doing peaceful protests is a serious thing. You have to fight with your biggest heart for the smallest hope for what is right. Somethings you might want to fight for would be for being treated fairly, being equal, saving animals, not littering and even more!

During the civil rights movement, black people started to be treated well. The world now has fewer servants but more money, and they have more freedom and harmony. Without civil rights, the world would be miserable. It would be miserable for the black people whose ancestors were slaves. White people forced them to be their servants! If you were a black person, how would you feel? White people would probably stop this once they imagined themselves in all the black people's places.

We are very glad that people have changed this racism. If the world were like this forever, I predict that the earth would soon turn what you call very miserable. Civil rights make the world better.

You don't need to try making your future better. Your future is better once you stop making your future better. Let God change it. Let your life stay how it is. Stay who you are and stay how you like. We are all trying to change the world. With civil rights, people changed the world. With just a little more help, we can make the world a better place, have better friends, and enjoy better lives. No matter what badness is out there, we can change the world. And a great example is civil rights! Do you want someday to show the world that you have the right feelings in your heart? Well, that might be a big job, but it may be easy when you have hope. Defending civil rights is a big role. We can make the world better by doing more good, just like the civil rights leaders I mention above did. But for now, I might want to stay where and what I am.

Essay 20: How to Help Animals

My topic for today will be "how to help animals." Have you ever wanted to help an animal? Well, in helping animals, you play an important role. It's not that hard if you know about this or that animal's issues. It depends on what animal you are choosing to help.

One way you can get the attention of people whose help you want would be at your school. How this works is as follows: you will gather all your friends at a place and tell them all about saving animals and what you want from them. Discuss this topic for a few minutes and try persuading them to help you. Once you have enough people, you should go to the school when recess ends and tell your teacher all about it. (Try being persuasive since some teachers don't like listening to their students). Once your teacher mutters "yes," you will decide what animal you would save and Google some ways to save the animal you choose.

For example, I would choose to help turtles. Turtles are becoming endangered because of people. People are throwing plastic bags in the ocean. Turtles bubble talk, saying that, when the plastic bag floats in the water, it may look like a jellyfish. Turtles eat jellyfish, but when they see a plastic bag, they might think that it will taste like a jellyfish. People could fix this problem by trying to throw fewer plastic bags away. So, in this way, having to fix animal issues is a great role. Sometimes it can even take two years to help animals.

Another example of an animal to help would be the great Chinese salamander. This animal is endangered because people are hunting this animal in China all the time to eat it. There are only a few left, so we should try to help them.

Animals play a big role in this environment since some animals have special features that help them help the world. Llamas patrol farms, narwhals are assistants to scientists, birds can make food, and sharks eat dead fish so diseases don't affect other fish, and other animals can help the earth too.

We should be helping too. The animals help the world while we help the world to help the animals and even other humans. Whenever you hear about animals being hurt, be quick to action! Depending on what animal you are caring for, you might try to help an animal but end up in a disaster. For instance, even driving your car to go help an animal, you're adding pollution to the environment! How to fix this problem? By getting more people to help you! The more help you get, the more you accomplish. GUARANTEED!

Essay 21: How Animals Help the World

My topic for today is how to save animals. Have you ever thought that animals were an inconvenience? Well, if you did, I say that is not true. Some animals that almost made the world perfect would be dogs, squirrels, rats and way more.

Now let me tell you some animals that are very useful to the earth. Rats are a big part of your life since even though you might think that they are animals that spread malaria and yellow fever, they also have something good in their life. They can smell out landmines! Starting from the civil war to World War II, people have been suffering from landmines that are hidden in the grass. Whenever you step on a landmine, you will explode!

Another animal that has made a big difference to the earth would be the dog. Dogs are role models for people, even now. How they helped the earth would be that they have been protecting animals. For example, some dogs protect cows so they stay in the herd. Or a different dog actually protects penguins.

Well, if you were an animal, what would you do to help the world? If it's hard for you to think of a way, try thinking of a way being human would help the earth. If I were an animal, I would help the environment in many ways. It depends on what characteristics you have. If you were a butterfly, you would likely be able to save the world by pollinating flower after flower. If you were a shark, you would help the environment by eating dead fish so that the dead fish don't quickly spread a disease in the water! It all depends on your features and your body shapes.

Basically, every animal on earth did something to make the world a better place. From the weakest to the strongest, the smallest to the biggest, all animals can do something to help the world. It all depends on their body shapes and what features they have.

If you would like an example, here's one. Penguins have white bellies while they have black backs. That helps the penguins. If you were a penguin and you were swimming, your white belly will look like the water since the light is facing down where it is very light. This camouflage makes the penguin invisible in the water. And same as on the back. On the back, things usually are dark. And since the back of a penguin is black, they can camouflage. This natural advantage helps the penguins stay safe from predators.

Now let's flip to the other flipper hand. What can we do as humans? Or as a human? Well, helping animals while being a human takes a lot of patience, decisions and steps. For the first step, you have to choose an animal that you would like to help. Your second step is when you start listing ways of how you can save this animal. Lastly, you will have to speak up to your parents into getting them to help you. Well, I hope now you have learned that animals are a big part of our world.

Essay 22: Saving the World

My topic for today is learning from the globe. Many people are trying to make their lives better by thinking of ideas and using them, but mostly many people try to make their lives better, but end up making trouble for the earth. We should be role models for the young people. We should make the world what it's supposed to be. Earth is supposed to support life, shelter, triumph, food and especially friends.

Some things that people have been doing that have ended up in disaster include smoking, which is bad for the earth since it has already caused a lot of trouble like being one cause of global warming, which makes the atmosphere get thinner and can make the polar bears and penguins and other animals that live in the North and South Poles die.

Another form of pollution that has caused many bad problems is littering. Have you ever seen people in their cars folding a paper airplane and when they're finished, they open the car window and throw it out to watch it glide in the sky? You might think that might not make anything bad since it is just one paper airplane, but actually that's not true. People are already throwing away a lot of garbage. When you throw it away, it will end up where all the rest of garbage is. You might think that you can throw away a lot of garbage, but think how it would look like in the place that has all of the garbage. My brain is giving me a picture of a place filled with garbage! Garbage is bad for the world too since it can cause a kind of liquid that is very toxic. This liquid can even make things explode! This liquid forms when garbage touches water for a long time.

Since now you know some things that have harmed the world, let's talk about things that will make the world even better than before. Using less paper would be one idea since you know that paper is made of bark, actually, so using less paper would save the trees in this environment. Driving less would also help the environment since if you drive a lot, you can cause global warming too. Instead, you should walk or use your bicycle. One of my most favourite ways to save our environment is to conserve water. This means saving water. Some ways you can save water is by taking fewer baths and taking shorter showers. All of these measures we can take to help improve our world.

Essay 23: Anywhere in the World

If I could live anywhere in the entire world, I would choose Tanzania! I'd look at all the lions and snakes and travel around all its wonderful places. I'd spend two weeks there with my friend, Emily. We'd see how people cook there, how they travel to places, and what kind of transportation they use. I'd find the comfiest hotel there and jump on all the beds! I'd sing: "I am sixteen, going on seventeen" with all my might. The song goes like this: "You are sixteen, going on seventeen, baby, it's time to think."

Next stop, I'd feel like eating an appetizing snack of pancakes. Guess where they are? In France! So here I go, to France! In France, I'd probably go to a shop or two since I know that the clothes there are so fancy! I'd choose skirts, dresses, blouses, and high heel shoes (oh-la-la). I'd finish all my homework, so I'd be totally finito. If I had any free time, I'd be sitting on the porch and daydreaming till I was at La-la Land. I would also go to the Eiffel Tower!

Next, I would go to... drum rollllllll... New York! I would mostly spend all that time in New York by watching shows like the Nutcracker. With a zip zap zoo, I'd be going from shop to shop carrying big bags of sweets and fashion clothes, going to museums and sightseeing and so much more! If it were winter, I'd be figure skating everywhere and showing off my axel jumps, Biellmann and back spins to everyone! If it were autumn, I would be making the biggest leaf pile in my entire life. When finished, I would run and leap into my leaf pile! If it were summer or spring, I'd like to go to get some ice cream before my next class starts. After two weeks in New York, I would go somewhere else—please do another drum rolllllllll.

I would like to go to... China. I'd love to go to my house and dress up in fancy clothes (secretly, in my mom's closet!). I'd dress up like a movie star wearing star-shaped glasses and make up; for example, eyeshadow, lip gloss, and smelly perfume. Then I would spend all my time climbing the Great Wall of China. After that, I would be exhausted, so I would buy some ice tea from a shop close to my hotel. After some drinks of ice tea, I would want to call my best friend for a play date. My friend and I would paint our nails all red, orange, yellow, green, indigo, aquamarine, violet, sapphire, and so much more! After all the nail polish, I would decide to go get some milk for my cat and much more! After the rock star show in my mom's closet, I would go get my nail polish set and cat named Marigold. Her last name is Pansies. After feeding Marigold, it would be time for me to say hello to my dad because he was back from work and bye to my friend because she was going to go to her house. After staying in China for two... (the speaker has just fallen asleep—Pedro, the library angel).

Part 4: Essays by Elaine

Part 4: Essays by Elaine

Essay 1: Environment

Our effects on the environment are causing a big problem.

First, let's start with the basics. What exactly is the environment? This is a question that we should answer in order to solve our problem. The environment is a big source of nature which helps us by giving us many useful substances.

How do we harm the environment? We harm it by making global pollution! Now, let's find out more about this problem.

What is pollution? Pollution is a toxic gas that can kill many animals and the environment. If the environment were to die, then humans, animals, and plants would have no food or water. We would all die, and the Earth would turn into a lifeless planet.

What is the cause of global warming? We make global warming by fuel burned by cars. Crude oil is especially used for fuel. When the smoke comes out of the ignition pipes, it rises up to the atmosphere, a protective shield around Earth. Then, the gas breaks through the atmosphere and floats into space, leaving a hole in our ozone layer. Without it, the heat would be very strong and would melt the polar ice caps, and the polar bears would have nowhere to live. Also, the extra water would create a flood, exactly the opposite of the Dust Bowl.

We don't have to stop driving cars. We should drive less, get in buses, or simply walk! That can help restore balance in the natural world. That is how we are affecting the environment, but saving it can be simple!

Essay 2: Covid-19

Why should we stay safe during the Covid-19 period? On this question, everyone should agree when talking about health safety. Over nearly the past year, Covid-19 has affected many people. Here are a few tips to keep you safe during Covid-19.

First, let's talk about the dangers of Covid-19. This virus has killed many people, including not only many in China but in every country on the planet. To prevent yourself from catching it, wearing a mask is always a good idea. A mask can protect your nose and mouth from invading airborne viruses.

Viruses affect your body first by getting into your body through a wound, your nose, your mouth, and/or your eyes. Then, once in, the virus starts attacking your body cells which try to fight back. The white blood cells defending the other cells clash against the virus with the help of antibiotics. If the white blood cells win, then you are not sick. Then, body symptoms start to manifest. The most common body symptoms are fevers, dry coughs, and exhaustion.

Masks work by providing an outer layer of defence of your body. You can usually distinguish a protective mask from a common decorative one, as it has a bendable wire over the nose, two ear loops on either side of the mask, and sometimes, plain blue or pink decorations.

Doctors especially have to wear masks because they work with people suffering from illnesses. Notably, the elderly need masks because they are weak and probably can't protect themselves from Covid-19.

The only solution to Covid-19 is to stay safe. So, we should do so at all costs. That is why we should stay safe during this Covid-19 pandemic. Staying safe during Covid-19 is very important and the only solution to this globally devastating disease.

Essay 3: War

The right reason to declare war is if someone else threatens a country and attacks it. It needs to defend itself, and someone can't just vote for peace if the fighting has already started. The country has to fight back.

Declaring war would be wrong if declared simply out of the desire for more land and money, and would be the act of greedy politicians and generals. Doing so made sense to absolute monarchs 400 years ago, but usually it was unreasonable.

If a government wants to prevent human abuses in another country by means of declaring war, that is rather dumb and wrong because causing more suffering is a terrible way of ending suffering. If a government thinks another country is getting too powerful, that is wrong because it has to wait until it attacks its own country to think so. You don't have to attack when someone else is harmed. This issue is linked to human abuses. If a country attacked your country, then someone is threatening you.

All of the reasons are connected but differ, some of them are right—some wrong! There is, then, a right and a wrong reason to declare war. That is why, if people want to declare war, their reason should be the right reason.

Essay 4: Choose Nature Over Technology

My topic for today is why technology is bad, even revolting in many ways.

The first reason I should mention involves taking care of yourself! Sometimes, watching TV will make you irritable, moody, and mean! You don't want that. To keep from having that happen, I suggest that you not watch TV all the time. It also causes sore eye muscles because staring at the screen too much will wear out your eyelids, and your eyes will become very droopy. Don't go watching your phone, computer, iPad, or any devices before going to bed. Staring at the light screen makes you think it's daytime, causing you to sleep very poorly because your brain is urging you to think that it's day, but you know it's time to sleep. Putting your phone near your bed can also cause poor sleep. Phones emit a blue light, sometimes white, causing poor sleep.

The next reason is that you need friends to live a good life! Imagine your life without friends. Dull, boring, alone, no one to encourage you... and friends are family! Then you're out, away from the TV, in... I don't know where—who knows? The woods, the desert—you name it! Spend more time in nature, don't watch the TV, and so on. Try to be natural!

Now, we want to talk about why being in nature is good. Sometimes, children, teenagers, and even adults feel freer in nature. Have YOU ever played in your yard or neighbourhood and felt so free you wanted to sing? I have, and you should too! We feel free because we are nature. If it hadn't been for nature, the human population wouldn't have been born.

Giraffes' tongues would not be blue. If it hadn't been for nature, the animals wouldn't be here. If it hadn't been for nature, there would be nothing! The colour green is also good for your eyes because green relaxes eye muscles.

Every day, week, month, and year, your choices depend on you. Whatever your choice is, ALWAYS, always, always, choose nature over technology.

Essay 5: My Favourite Job

My favourite job would be to work as an engineer. Not to fix things, but to make objects that inspire me.

The only object that inspires me to be an engineer is a Lego hummingbird! This bird started with patience. I was trying to make something out of Lego. I just got a new idea to make a hummingbird, and my mind was spinning! I fiddled until I was sweating, finishing everything, and I smiled. The hummingbird was done! That was how I discovered that I wanted to be an engineer. Also, I could easily imagine how it would work. In my opinion, to make something new is the best way to learn. Did you know that all scientists, engineers, and chemists who want to learn something new, learn it by experiencing something that is happening to them? It's true! I want to learn things I want to know more about! If you are confused, then take a look at this example: my favourite pastime (the hobby I like to do in my free time) is to try finding out how something works.

Time and discovery have a link. That bond is very strong because:

1. Time is linked to discovery because it takes time to discover new knowledge.

2. Discovery is linked to time because discovery is a big flash of time speeding up.

3. Literally, we learn new things in our dreams and thoughts throughout days and months.

4. The many discoveries we hold in ourselves do not fade as we die.

5. The world is a treasure map and every step we make offers the secrets that we take along down another path until we die.

Every obstacle we face is a big opportunity in that time of discovery. That is what I think about discovery, and this is the best way for me to be an engineer of simple discoveries.

Essay 6: My Greatest Fear

My greatest fear—death, always takes me over at night, making me clammy with sweat as I think about the subject. Just the thought of it makes me shiver. Death has always scared me. Just imagine not ever being able to see anything or think anything again! The blackness at night also makes me think about what it will look like when I die.

Sometimes, I try thinking of Gods and heaven to make me feel better. Believing in these myths is hard though because if they were (or are) there, why don't they show a sign? Wanting people to represent them, they have to show a sign!

It's hard to believe others who say that dying is common. I don't know if they're not scared of dying or if they like dying. It just makes me worried! I've searched in Google why death is not scary although the results still don't convince me. Even looking at dead people is scary. Often, their eyes are open, and they look as if suddenly they will be able to come alive, grab me, and cast me in Tartarus (I am not convincing; I am informing).

I try to sleep better, exercise more, eat full meals, and so on. It doesn't help! I hope you understand my top fear of death, and I hope you are now fully informed!

Essay 7: Saving the Endangered Ones

We should save endangered animals from becoming extinct. Animal extinction is caused by air and water pollution, global warming, and littering.

Imagine if you were about to be extinct. That would be like living nowhere, in a world with nothing, such as living on Mars, all alone. With nothing, you would feel sad. When you feel too alone, soon you would lose the will to live, but by that time, your species will already be extinct.

Perhaps your neighbour or father loves a kind of species like the great pandas, but they are already on the endangered list because their habitats are being destroyed. Many other animals are very, very interesting although they might become endangered in the future.

Talking of that, we can wonder if we would like it if a big thing ploughed through our homes and got a big noisy loud thing and went raiding about? We are talking about how it would be for the grasshoppers, ladybugs, butterflies, caterpillars, spiders, houseflies, and many more! Those numbers of pests may seem harmful even though they are sometimes helpful and scare away other pests such as the spider eats mosquitoes or the wasp eats ants. Many pests may be enemies or friends, but most of them are enemies. Imagine them in your yard and trying to scramble away as the lawn mower destroys their homes. They are not used to having you mow your yard, so they have not adapted to it.

Also, think about the food chain as being kind of like a maze. The top ones are not always the sharks or the bears; instead, it's us. We usually eat sharks' fins. The food chain starts with plankton, and then goes to fish, then seals, and then people. The food chain mostly splits off because an animal has more than one enemy. That enemy has an enemy, and so on.

How are we destroying the populations of animals? We may think it is no harm at all, just a natural form of killing, but really, species extinction is a big change. Usually, the food chain comes to us, but the human species could also become extinct if we don't have food to eat. The consequences are very sad. We have become the enemies of monkeys. And after they become extinct, we will become extinct too. We won't come back again because there are no apes to recreate us. And our population will be over.

To wrap up my essay, let me say I hope you are convinced to save the endangered ones, to bring them back from the brink of extinction, to vote and act to stop pollution and to help the environment.

Essay 8: The Library

My topic for today is how library class is a VERY good class!

Now, you might think that library class is the worst class since some people can't write while others love to fall asleep there. Yet, although some people don't like to write, they love to draw and read instead. Now, one of those people who loves the library is me! Library class is a good class because reading can make you smart. Non-fiction AND fiction can make you clever and intelligent. In reading realistic fiction, you can learn a lesson because, in some books, there is a problem to be solved. d bit his cheek! The lesson in that book is to be cautious before you do something. Now, that's not all! Then the character or characters might make a good choice! And then the character or characters get out of trouble! Big puffy cheeks, for example. This character was hanging around in the desert with his shoes off. A scorpion climbed up his legs, nothing naughty.

Non-fiction can make you smart by the teaching it gives you. Imagine you read a book about plants. Then the next day, you had to write an essay about plants. And then when you hand in your essay, you might have a good mark because you read that book!

Anyway, reading can also make you think deeply about something. Imagine that you got a VERY interesting book and you were engrossed in it. That way, you would have something to be mindful of.

These, then, are some of my reasons for loving library classes!

Essay 9: Machines

My topic for today is what machine I would like to invent! Of course, you might think that only adults are allowed to make machines, but actually children can make machines too!

My machines are called TwiceTime, CountCits, and StretchSnake!

The first one, TwiceTime, is a little decorated bowl that can turn one thing into two of the same thing! Imagine that you wanted to make a gingerbread house. You only had one green jelly bean, one yellow skittle, one brown M&M, one piece of dark chocolate, one stick of pink gum, one tuft of purple cotton candy, one rainbow lollipop, one piece of beige gingerbread, one small chocolate chip, one chocolate chip cookie, one blue and red gummy worm, one piece of red liquorice, and one silver gummy bear! But you needed twenty of all of those. If you use TwiceTime, then your problem is solved!

The CountCits is a little calculator. Imagine that you wanted to know how many grains of sand were in your hands. You put the calculator on top of the grains of sand, and then the calculator shows how many grains of sand there are.

The StretchSnake is a little ball that is designed like a unicorn, but the machine is not so useful because it isn't used much. The machine has a button that says stretch, and when you press it, it uncurls and turns into a very, very, very, very, very, very, very, very long stick. At the end of the stick, there are pincers like the pincers on an ant, except way, way, bigger. At the front, there is a button and the writing on it says "close".

When you press the button, the pincers close. When you let go of the button, the pincers open.

Now that I have told you about some of my machines, why don't you start brainstorming new machines yourself?

Essay 10: Spring

My topic for today is that spring is a season of life! That is because animals such as bears and deer come out from their dens and play and have babies. Flowers start blooming, flowers such as daffodils yellow and fair, daisies as soothing as angels, buttercups as yellow angels that bring back sentimental memories, dandelions sparkling like the sun, roses as red as rubies, leaves as fresh as emeralds, stems as strong as wire, sunflowers as brown as wood, wood as smooth as chocolate, bees buzzing and busy like businessmen, ants swarming like sand, breezes that are soft and welcoming like a pillow, bluebells clear like the sea, laughter all around the place, popsicles cold and calm, and sunsets colourful and calm like a rainbow. And if I forgot to tell you, these are all reminders of spring!

It is a season of life because lots of spring animals come out, animals such as deer, chipmunks, rabbits, birds, butterflies, lambs, bears, and dragonflies! Birds chirp and sing, deer come out and play, butterflies flit and flutter, and children laugh and play! Birds come out to lay their eggs; it is perhaps their favourite time of the year! They have laid eggs in the spring because there are more worms and caterpillars to feed the baby birds! The caterpillars and worms are alive, and are letting the birds eat them because the worms and caterpillars are busy eating the leaves and dirt. The plants need sun and dirt to live! And fertilizer helps the dirt to provide nutrition for the plants! Also, fertilizer is made out of our organic waste so the birds are eating our organic waste!

After all this splendour, magnificence, and excellence, I'm convinced that you will think that spring is a season of life, although there is more! It's also a season of life because that's when you're most willing to live! Also, that's the same as least wanting someone to die. So now, I think you learned why spring is a season of life!

Essay 11: Ice Cream Sundae World

One day, I went outside, and all of the grass and trees had turned into an ice cream sundae world. What was the first thing I did?

I ate all of the creamy cold plants at home. Then I went outside to go skating, but the ice was too thin, and I knew that I'd just fall through the ice instead. So, I tried to walk on the ice, but it began to crack and break, just as I suspected. I tried to walk off the ice, but my skates were glued to it. So, I took the scissors from my pocket, and I had bad news. The scissors were frozen!!! So, I decided to call 911. Minutes later, the next door police came. They tried their scissors, but their scissors were also frozen. Ding!!! An idea popped into my mind!

I asked, "Can I have some alone time, please?"

They said, "Yvonne, your sis will accompany you."

So, they left me, and my sister Yvonne came.

She said, "Why do you need my help?"

I answered, "It's because I need you to help me break the ice by munching and eating ice!"

And then we munched together on the ice until... CRACK!!! I fell through the ice (I didn't really fall since Yvonne grabbed my arm just in time).

"So, pull me up!" I said to Yvonne, and she did. I asked her, "Are you hungry?"

She replied, "Of course."

So, we went into my house, and I told Yvonne to wait in the dining room. I went outside to gather ten leaves, twenty blades of grass, and four tiny or medium trees. I brought them into the house, and I used Yvonne's help to separate the ten leaves into two fives, the twenty blades of grass into two tens, and finally but not last, we took two little trees for our own. Then we took the two piles and put one pile on my plate, and the other one on Yvonne's. After a great feast, we went home. But when I lay down on my bed in my outside clothes, I realized that I didn't change. So, I quickly jumped out of my bed and changed into my pyjamas and hopped back into bed, fell fast asleep, dreaming that tomorrow morning would be the same good day.

Part 5: Poems by Yvonne

Thanksgiving

Thanksgiving is a wonderful day, as you know, as many people celebrate appreciation for their family and friends.

Though we talk about this, Thanksgiving is the day when family and family, sibling and sibling go together as a family celebrates together to let each other know they appreciate the help they were given.

Mothers serve turkey and chicken to their kids and they drool as they watch their mother cook a wonderfully fabulous dinner.

Schools share what they are most grateful for during Thanksgiving, making crafts like cards for saying thank you or for telling them you are grateful for them to be helping you.

Thanksgiving is a time of harvest as many do gather, helping farmers pick food such as berries and fruit, pumpkins and more.

On Thanksgiving, help is provided here and there as people together fixing each other's problems.

Now, all of you must be mindful of dessert! The tasty treats melt in your mouth like warm water pouring in a cup, and you taste the delectable but fragile flavour of your favourite dessert.

You would always help in the kitchen to cook, smelling the ginger, peeling oranges, and helping your parents to prepare dinner.

Black Friday! That's the last day of Thanksgiving! Families gather again and of course go shopping for presents and stuff they need.

At school, teachers teach kids to sing autumn songs or songs related to the harvest of the food; families gather and enjoy many other activities that many people do to celebrate Thanksgiving.

Schools skip Monday to let kids relax and celebrate Thanksgiving while they commemorate together at school, all having fun.

Autumn Celebration

The leaves have turned red, yellow, and brown, standing out like a painting we are living in.

The wind has grown and we can hear the hushing of the trees turning and twisting in the morning wind.

We are staying inside more as cold weather has woken up from the clouds and sun down for autumn.

Pumpkins are disappearing—busy shoppers buying them up to celebrate Halloween night.

Kids are blasting off ideas about what to be on Halloween night.

Ideas spreading fast and steady as kids slowly and carefully choose their costumes.

Candy is delivered here and there as children stuff their mouths with delectable candy, thinking that was a glorious night.

Pranks are played while little friends scare each other, laughing and also enjoying the joy of Halloween.

The nights stay silent, only the hooting of an owl to be heard.

Contests on the best pumpkin carvers start as marvellous pictures are carved into pumpkins, nice and neat as each competitor wants to win.

Schools go crazy as kids are scared, showing off their most fabulous costumes in pride, hoping to be the best.

Families celebrate together, having a great time chatting and eating, full with joy as everyone is happy for all.

At school, students sing the noise of owls and creeping music fills their ears when they hear the haunted music of Halloween.

Children start to go to camp while kids choke with creepy stories, trying to scare somebody with their creepy stories, crawling down their brain like spiders crawling on to their hands.

It's easy to predict when it's going to rain, and the weather is going to be bad as you watch the grey clouds storming in, and you hear the pitter-patter of rain as the joy of a sunny day is crushed.

We carve funny faces on our pumpkins, while some seem scary and some possibly scare others enough for them to jump back and screech, while a bunch of other kids laugh as the owner of the pumpkin is the leader of the group, showing how she or he did it and walking with the high happy head of the leader.

Some kids daydream they are explorers ready to venture into a cave full of bats, blood sucking bats, glowing like bioluminescent fungi or mushrooms, glow-in-the-dark shrubs or white larva shining bright blue.

Fireflies glow like fire buzzing all around us, life-flashing lanterns and flying around, trying to find a female to mate with, while other fireflies flash messages to each other, like typing on Skype to your friends, one after another, having a good time chatting.

Adults let their kids go to the graveyard to look at the people in their family who have died to bring peace, respect, and love to them, to let them know that even though they aren't here, they still make a difference to their families, their lives and others, and their families will always remember them.

Another activity I enjoy a lot is picking pumpkins in the pumpkin patch.

How I Made A Raft

In the breezy wind, we stand together.
The whisper of the rustling trees running through my hair.
The sun, like a crystal ball shining on the earth of life, creates the clouds to float, the sea to sparkle, and the bees to hum a tune of life.
I sway along to the hum of the wild, the grass feeling like cotton under my feet, the smell of mint all around me.
The fragrance is delicate but sensational, like the master's Song of Myself.
A smell of honey and the life of earth. The flowers bloom and stand as if magic is about to awaken.
The sky is filled with dreams that float all around me.
The white moon starts to shine, and the stars start to dazzle,
Shooting stars doing their job when a wish comes true one by one.
The sky darkens as we await a song or howl of a mourning wolf.
As the sun rises, we hear the chirping of birds, the morning sway of a dance of macrabray!
This is the time when you have to wake, you have to wake.
I feel the sunshine on my face as I go down as if in a race.
I eat my breakfast as normally we do; I hide outside and feel the tide.
The feeling of water races through my bones as I watch the rapid fish swimming all around me.
The corals open up here and there as their welcoming colours awaken fish and attract the seabirds!

Feeling the strong currents of the water, I wade even more; I stop next to a sea star heading to shore.

The sea has many wonders which I don't know, but I use each clue to find each creature.

The sand feels soft under my feet, the breeze never this strong before, so I'm going to make a raft.

Swift enough to follow the crashing current and big enough to fit a cow.

I start with a woollen sail, big and white, swift and soft to make a sleeping loft.

Next, strong sticks longer than the sail, all smooth and tight, steady and stable.

Lastly, a bunch of sticks strung together to make the raft fast and easy.

Put the smooth sail around those large sticks, my mast, and upright in the middle of the raft.

Deciding it to be a ravishing raft, I would have signed it as a final draft!

The sun having started to set, I hear the goodbyes of the sun. I run back to my home and will start a new day tomorrow.

Christmas Time

Christmas evening has come.

The trees have turned white, and everything we see around us is glittering with white snow.

The tree has already been settled in its place, decorated, and the evening when children mingle round and round like dust floating in the air is underway.

The parents are smiling as the children's laughter fills the air, flying through the house on Christmas Eve.

Everyone seems to be mingling, happy and passionate to have a good time.

Giggles take some part while laughter takes another; the delicate scent of mint fills the room.

The mistletoe hanging joyfully on the tree, seems to make everybody feel free!

The fire has started as the warmth spreads free, the love spreading together like a contagious laugh.

We all know the feeling of getting a present, so, as you usually know, Christmas is a time of presents when you give presents one by one, as everyone oohs and ahhs together, looking at what they got.

Getting a new watch, some craft materials, money, or anything you wish!

Christmas evening brings a fun smell of mint, the smiles of adults, the laughter of kids, and presents given early.

The cake is ready, we are ready too, to celebrate Christmas Eve, the snow shining like crystals and the ice that used to be grass is starting to melt from the heat from the fireplace.

Ding, ding, ding!

The sound of the bell heralds dinner is ready for everyone to eat.

Parents stop mingling as they hurry to wash with soap that smells like ginger.

The kids squeal in excitement to see what's for dinner on this fabulous winter evening.

The table is brown and strong as can be, as the decorated cloth is all covered by hand-painted poinsettia, nice and neat.

The most spectacular part is yummy food, the dishes I counted that all three servants made for us: apple cloves, coriander fish, and fresh vegetables, mint-scented cakes.

The snow is descending everywhere outside the warm house.

Part 6: Poems by Elaine

My Heart

My heart only goes thump, thump, thump.
If you open me up, it looks like a lump!
It's mostly red, clotting where I bled; my heart
is the best, never needing to rest.
It never wants to leave, just helps me breathe,
which makes it strong, its beat never wrong.
It tells me the time; it always makes a rhyme,
and if it has eyes, don't let it be seized!
When will it know, it doesn't have to row, in
a sea of red, where it is being led?
It isn't helpless goo, doesn't go to the loo,
because it doesn't know who, it is led to!
If it could see, whenever that will be, I just
guarantee, it is a she who will get a degree!
Does it know why, it can't just cry; it will
just have to sigh—I just can't reply!
It doesn't have a mouth because it has
too much youth; it will turn south.
It will feel like a feather, as smooth as leather—whatever!
Every day, it's like a ray, for where it lays is stronger than clay.
It's as small as a fist where two genes
kissed—its pulse is in the wrist.
Working like a phone, it is alone, better than
a bone; it should take the throne!
It makes your emotions stop all commotion,
just like a healing lotion!
It has the right to work at night as pure as white!

Upon much blood, it is beloved, not to be judged.
Just right for its career, nothing is unclear, that it is sincere.
As good as new, it can go into everything true.
Everyone knows, from hair to toes,
that every day, it has a rose.
From week to month, everyone knows
that it won't punch anyone's lunch!

My Recipe for A Friend:

Ingredients:
3 tsp of silliness
4 pinches of jokes
5 tbsp of connection
2 cups of kindness
1 big bowl of friendship
1 cup of comfort
4 cups of tolerance
9 tsp of unique talents
2 big bowls of simple love
3 cups of calmness
9 cups with forgiveness
1 eyedropper of food colouring (optional)
1 rainbow
3 cups total of sprinkles, marshmallows, and ground-up mint

Materials: A big bowl, a tray, a shaper, and an oven.

Instructions:

Mix silliness and jokes together to make your friend humorous if you wish to do so. Knead the mixture, so your friend is funny. Dump connection in the mixture, so your friend's jokes make you feel included.

Pour kindness in a big bowl and add friendship. Knead until fluffy and sprinkle in comfort, so your friend gives you comfort.

Combine both mixtures. It should make a reddish-orange colour. As you knead the big lump, pour in tolerance and talent. Now, the mixture should be a light blue—indigo when raw.

Take one bowl of simple love. It should be white.

Leave both mixtures to dry for one hour. When you come back, it should be like honey: a slow, sticky liquid. The mixture in the big bowl should be like pink sand.

Mix both mixtures, along with calmness, and forgiveness in the tray.

You should have nothing left except an oven, a big bowl, a shaper, and three cups of sprinkles, marshmallows, and ground-up mint.

The mixture in the tray should be like clay. Add in food colouring until the eyedropper is empty. The mixture should be that colour.

Dump in sprinkles, marshmallows, and ground-up mint.

Now, put the mixture in the shaper.

Heat the oven up to 752 F. Put the shaper inside. After 15 minutes, take it out of the shaper.
Put under the rainbow, and the shape will spring to life, become a human, and turn into your friend!
Enjoy!

Acknowledgement:

We would like to thank Tellwell for giving us this opportunity to publish our earlier works, especially Sem Delima, the project manager, for his complete guidance and help. We also would like to thank Mei for her wonderful interior illustrations, and finally a big thanks to Mr. Duo Su for his artistic design of the book covers.